Beyond

a

Heartbeat

Beyond a Heartbeat

ASHNA KEDIA

Srishti
PUBLISHERS & DISTRIBUTORS

SRISHTI PUBLISHERS & DISTRIBUTORS
Registered Office: N-16, C.R. Park
New Delhi – 110 019
Corporate Office: 212A, Peacock Lane
Shahpur Jat, New Delhi – 110 049
editorial@srishtipublishers.com

First published by
Srishti Publishers & Distributors in 2019

Printed at Repro Knowledgecast Limited, Thane

To my beautiful friends and family,
I am nothing without your support.

You define love.

1

November: First Year of IBII

'Indian Business Institute Indore,' I read on the gate of the entrance to my fairly old and extremely prestigious university. The lettering was big, bold and silver and it stood out in the small city of Indore. It did a magnificent job of reflecting light, making even the rusty gate – that was hung on its hinges at a jaunty angle – look deceptively glamorous. Amidst the nooks and crannies of the city, the lettering looked how I felt – like we didn't quite belong. I entered the gate sluggishly and signed in with my student credentials.

"Any guests?" the guard muttered.

"Not this time." I sighed.

I was a Delhi girl and I had lived in a cosy house in Malviya Nagar all my life until I had magically received the acceptance offer from IBII one day. It wasn't that I hadn't prepared for the entrance examination, but growing up hearing tales of my elders studying hours to get through had me expecting a rejection letter. I had always been inclined towards mathematics, and my love for reading ensured decent vocabulary. Inherent skills teamed up with a couple of half-hearted classes and practice tests had been enough to help me crack the exam. The interview round acted as a bonus to my confident and well-presented demeanour, and so, here I was, at the supposedly best institution for MBA in India.

Initially, I hadn't been sure if I was ready to uproot my life at home, but chances like these didn't come by twice. I loved my friends, my family and my routine back in Delhi, but my comforts fell short while weighing the advantages of studying in this institution. I would probably be earning in lakhs by the time I was done with this course at the mere age of twenty-three. A rational person wouldn't think twice and yet I felt nauseous at the thought of spending two years away from home.

As a child, I had imagined leaving home as one of the most exhilarating experiences in a teenager's life. I had wondered whether my parents would tear up at the thought of their baby finally leaving the nest. As I had closed my door for the last time, I had run my hand along the handle. Skinny at the edges and thick in the middle, I memorized the way the cold steel felt against my palm. Just the thought of not using the door I had used since I was a child was enough to bring me to tears. I had balled up all my memories in my chest, carrying their weight around me wherever I went.

I had enrolled in August and it had only been three months, but I took up every opportunity to fly back home.

"It's her birthday," I would whine to my mum about some friend I hadn't spoken to for months.

We both knew the game I was playing at, but she let me book tickets anyway, feeling sorry for my lonesome soul. Every visit back to Delhi left a void in my heart when I was eventually forced to return. I looked forward to any long weekend that could allow me to be with everyone I loved for a few more days.

Ours was a small nuclear family and I lived with both my parents, and my sister. My mum and dad used to work for long hours when I was younger and that meant that growing up, I spent most of my time with my nanny and my sister, Radhika. Later, my dad retired and started depending on his pension. My mother also switched to a less hectic work plan and their number one priority suddenly became the family. They put in tremendous effort organising game nights and picnics for the four of us, planning the location and the food days in advance. Despite their best attempts, families tend to argue and these events only had a fifty percent chance of success. There were days when Radhika and I would be interactive, giving the family all our attention. There would also be days when these events felt forced and we behaved like grumpy and distracted teenagers throughout. Coming here, I realized that I missed game night terribly, and I couldn't wait to go back again and work on my Taboo skills. We spent so many evenings bickering about the usage of synonyms and the number of negative points when a taboo word was used that we had to come up with a functional system based on personalised ground rules to avoid family fights. My mother hated to lose almost as much as I did, and us teamed up against one another always ensued fiery arguments of all sorts. Radhika and my dad acted like referees and tried to be as impartial as they could be. As kids, Radhika took my side incessantly, while my dad took my mum's, but she had now switched to my mum's side, forcing my dad to take mine. Our fights were chaotic and noisy, but I enjoyed fighting with them more than talking to most people here.

I looked at the dreary academic block building looming over me. One of the upsides to being in this university was that Radhika had been preparing meticulously to crack the exam and would join me the following year, I hoped. The other upside was Aryan. He was just a boy I had met once, but something about him had left me intrigued. I was completely content not being in a relationship, but he had planted a seed of hope in my mind for a more interesting future in IBII.

Aryan was also from Delhi, but unlike me, he wasn't finding fitting in troublesome. He had already become quite popular amongst our batch and I often saw girls admiring him from afar. We didn't have many classes in common, and in the beginning, I hadn't felt much inclination to talk to him, or anyone else for that matter. My only goal had been to get out of this institution as fast as I could and pray that Radhika would join me soon.

As a blessing in disguise, Aryan had stood behind me one day in October while I waited in the queue for food in the mess. I had had a rough day, starting with being late for my financial strategy class. Sameer sir threw quite a fit and thoroughly succeeded in embarrassing me in front of the other sixty students. I blamed the hundred-and-fifty acre campus with no means of transportation, besides walking. He blamed the city I came from. He didn't care for my 'excuses' and felt no remorse in calling me a spoilt Delhi girl. He was also one of the few teachers whom I looked up to and respected. He had an outstanding educational background and had done his master's from Stanford. He had a great command over mathematics and finance and taught the subjects passionately. I took being insulted by him even more personally than I would with any other authoritative figure.

In no mood to talk, I had been checking my phone and idly looking at Snapchat stories of my friends, wondering what I would be doing if I were anywhere but here.

"Hey, isn't that the lane with all the embassies near Chanakyapuri?" Aryan had asked, peeking at my phone.

"Do you usually look into other peoples' phones?" I had replied sourly.

He had looked at me sheepishly and said, "I'm sorry, I couldn't help it. I live close to that lane and I figured that you must be from Delhi as well. It's always nice talking to my own people."

I had no other friends and this could do no harm. I forced a smile and introduced myself.

"Hey, I'm Raina Kapoor. So far, I have no idea what I'm doing here."

"Hi Raina, I'm Aryan Malik and I can help you with that!" he had said grinning with infectious energy.

"How do you manage to be so upbeat while waiting to be served daal and rice?"

"Look for the silver lining, Raina. It's only a matter of two years and then you could be eating at my restaurant."

"You have a restaurant? What are you doing here then?"

"Correction, I want a restaurant and I'm pretty damn sure I'm going to get it."

"I happen to love good food, so I'm sure we'll get along fine."

"Oh, I hope my palate is upto your mark then," Aryan had said nudging me playfully.

I had spent the rest of dinner with him and found myself unexpectedly enjoying his company. He had felt like a piece of home in the forlorn IBII. He had offered to walk me to the girls' dorm after dinner and I had appreciated his chivalry, especially after meeting the boys in this university. It felt like the men here had never even spent time with females other than the ones in their immediate families. If the stories of hard work required to get admission here were true, I was guessing they probably hadn't. Although they were sweet, they failed to pick up on social cues and some of them had asked me to be their girlfriend within an hour of meeting me. I even saw a guy whistle at a vaguely attractive girl to get her attention. I hope for her sake that she didn't end up dating him.

Once Aryan had dropped me back, I had climbed yet another flight of stairs and thought about whether we would talk again. It sounded like a cliché, but it was endearing how Aryan was attractive without knowing it. His goofiness was charming and warmth radiated from him like the sun. He had treated me as if I were an old friend and not just someone he had run into for the first time at a canteen and I appreciated his efforts to make me feel included.

As I walked to my dorm, lugging my suitcases behind me, I vaguely looked forward to seeing Aryan again. It wasn't like me to ponder over a guy, but I didn't have much else to look forward to. Amidst all the grey clouds, I wondered if he would be my silver lining.

2

Classes continued and I didn't see much of Aryan after that unexpected night in October. I was bombarded with an immense workload that I had to somehow finish by the end of the week. My books were lying around me and I was glad I had a room where I could be messy. There was nobody to stop me from playing my music and I was allowed to shut myself off to focus at my own convenience. A roommate wouldn't have been a bad idea for when it got lonely, but I remembered sharing a room with Radhika and that had definitely put a strain on our relationship. Although we had our separate rooms, we had excitedly decided to share mine and had innocently thought that every night would be a sleepover. At first, I was willing to give her half of everything. Sure, she could have my wardrobe and bathroom space; she was my sister, after all. Yes, I could be quieter for her. Okay, she could use my phone when I wasn't in the room. Fine, I could live with her snoring. The constant sacrifice got on my nerves and we were soon arguing about petty things from the mess on the floor to who would charge the speakers at night.

"Radhika, I agreed to sleep early for you even though I wanted to practice for my dance show. The very least you could do is get up and turn the lights down!" I screamed at her.

"Raina, are you incapable of talking at a normal volume? Do something yourself. You know I had a test today and I'm really tired!"

We bickered and bickered until I finally couldn't take it anymore. My dear sister was dearer when she was down the corridor.

The rooms over here weren't as big as my room back in Delhi, but they were spacious enough for one person to live in comfortably. IBII had provided us with two cupboards, a bed, a mirror and a desk with a chair. We had also been given a few shelves that I adorned with my favourite novels of all time. The curtains were cherry red and white, and I had to admit that they didn't do a half bad job of brightening up the room. I had desperately tried to make my room homely by adding fairy lights and artificial potted plants. It had worked to an extent, but I had realized that no matter what I did, I couldn't trick myself into believing that the four walls were enough for me. I had brought along one picture with me and it stood proudly in its frame on my desk. Often, I gazed at it before falling asleep. It was a picture my entire family of four sprawled in our garden, content just being around each other. My grandmother had taken the picture, and although she counted as family, the family I had grown up with meant the most to me.

I willed myself to concentrate on the Finance book lying in front of me. We had to study for a quick test in class the day after and my love for numbers paired with my competitiveness motivated me to do well in quantitative courses. This course, in particular, had become the mathematical beast of our programme. Either way, I had to make up for my tiff with Sameer sir, and if buttering up didn't work, scoring well had to impress him. I had never been a teacher's pet, but my luck with teachers had gone down the drain here. I planned on being on good terms with him, especially considering his readiness to punish students for minute mistakes.

I massaged my throbbing temple, forcing myself to finish reading the last two pages of the topic at hand. Stifling a yawn, I tried to ignore the way the words had started to blur together. After a few hours of studying, I was satisfied with how thoroughly I knew the syllabus. I decided to take a shower in the common bathroom on my floor. Every floor had four bathrooms, which meant that each bathroom was shared by ten girls. Five cubicles amongst the ten of us seemed fair and we all did our share by not leaving any product or hair behind.

I walked into one of the cubicles and hoped that the hot water problem had been fixed. The water often took time to heat up and I took that time to set my bottles of shampoo and conditioner onto the bathroom shelf. I put my hand under the tap and was delighted to feel the warm water cascading through. I entered the shower and let the heat relax my body. The pressure gently massaged my tired muscles and I felt my body soften. Hot water showers had become my personal form of drugs on campus. Not that there was a lack of drugs in our university!

Students easily snuck in all sorts of substance to get themselves high or drunk or both. It was an easy escape from the bleakness of IBII. I had never been too inclined on anything that required smoking, being an asthmatic kid, but it fascinated me anyway. I often heard all sorts of stories from my friends back home and they told me all about the wonders of weed. It was supposed to be the grown up version of 'Hakuna Matata' which translated to having no worries. They told me about the calm and peace they felt once they had smoked up and encouraged me to give it a try. Giving in, I had tried inhaling a joint, but the smoke had clogged up my throat, causing me to cough like a maniac. Even though my friends had laughed and called me weak, I hadn't felt the need to smoke up after that instance, and that had been the end of my short-lived drug abuse. All part of the college experience, they say.

Getting out of the shower, I wrapped a towel around my body and walked to my room. There were a few grey pebbles lying outside my door. Was this really the idea of ragging here? I started collecting the pebbles when another pebble flew past me. Looking down, I found the culprit to be much cuter than I had imagined.

"Is this usually how you serenade girls, Aryan?" I laughed.

"Don't flatter yourself, I just didn't have your number, that's all."

"And did you happen to stumble across my room?"

"Okay, I asked around Raina. Just letting you know, not many people know your humble abode."

"What's so important that it couldn't wait until tomorrow morning?"

"Please, I've barely seen you in the last two weeks. Now, do you plan on coming downstairs or do you prefer this form of communication?"

"Give me a second."

I ran to my room and wrapped a scarf around my shoulders. The weather in Indore could get chilly at night and I liked to be prepared.

"Okay Raina, now listen to the plan. You and I both know that men aren't allowed in the girls' dorm. The guard wasn't there when I came in, but now she is, and you're going to have to help me sneak out," Aryan said with a mischievous grin.

I needed some excitement in my life and this seemed like an inviting idea.

"You're going to talk to the guard about any problem that you might have, but you'll have to take her further away. Meanwhile, I'll take the opportunity to run out of the building and you're going to join me on the football field in five minutes."

I walked up to the guard and quickly ran over ideas in my head that would force her to leave the building entrance.

"Didi, this is my second month here and I don't really know where the tuck shop is. We have a test tomorrow and I missed dinner, so I was hoping you could show me where it is. I'm really hungry and I need something to eat," I said hoping to strike with the sympathy card.

She looked around, probably scouting the safety of the area and then grunted in agreement. She walked me towards the direction of the tuck shop and gave me the required instructions for the route.

"Take a left and walk until you reach the computer block. Take a right from there and keep going on until you see a garden. After that, take another right and you'll see the tuck shop."

I made her repeat the directions, giving Aryan a few extra minutes to run out.

"Thank you so much, Didi. Would you like me to bring you something to eat as well?"

"No," she refused sternly.

I waited for her to go back to the dorm and then jogged to the football field. Calling the patches of grass a football field would be kind on the students' part, but I didn't play the sport, so it wasn't much of my concern. I looked around for Aryan, but he was nowhere to be seen. I nervously wondered if the guard had caught him and if he had given her my name. Sneaking a guy in or out couldn't possibly lead to expulsion, I hoped.

"Not bad, Raina!"

I heard Aryan's footsteps approaching.

"You seem to be a real pro at this sneaking out thing, Mr Aryan Malik."

"Oh, she remembers my name," he teased. "I've had my moments."

"Why is it that you've summoned me to the football field at this time of the night?"

"The night is young and I felt like catching up with you. Come, take a walk with me."

For the first time, the idea of walking around the massive campus didn't fill me with dread. I skipped over to him to catch up with his hasty pace. We spent the next hour strolling around the campus and he showed me the buildings I had never bothered to discover before. I learnt that our campus had a pool and made a mental note to go swimming soon.

As we sauntered, we discussed who we were as people and what had brought us here. Aryan told me about his dream restaurant and his love for food. He talked about how his mother, the engineer, made sure she cooked for their family every night. Most of the quality time he had spent with her was at this time, as they both were busy during daytime. He used to watch as she mixed spices and created new dishes, especially for him. They had a family rule of eating dinner together whilst they discussed how their respective days had been.

"Dinner always brought us together and it was what I looked forward to the most. I would hear Mumma-Papa's loving banter, and on the rare days Mumma made something I didn't like, I would sneak it under the table for my German Shepherd, Hunter. Later, I couldn't take out so much time from my busy schedule. I always had homework or football practice. On the days I didn't, I would go to my friends' houses to play Fifa or League of Legends. After school, clubbing became the new gaming, which meant that I was often out until late, but I always tried to spend at least a few dinners with them in a week. That's where my dream of owning a restaurant stems from."

"As the lugubrious lady invites her friends to her posh house for a fancy meal and the timid lad asks his lover to accompany him for dinner, we accept food not only to be a means of fulfilling dietary requirements, but also as a means of meeting loved ones over bread and candlelight," I absent-mindedly recited the lines from one of the books I had read in the previous summer. I realized that I may have sounded pretentious and I looked at him sheepishly.

"Exactly!" Aryan said, taking me by surprise.

"So, can you cook, or is your contribution limited to eating the food?"

"I don't usually boast, but since you asked, yes, I can cook really well. Although I am yet to reach the high standards my mother set," he smiled and I felt my knees shaking.

By the end of the night, we had spoken about everything under the sun. We had covered preferences in food, clothes, colours, books and music. We had debated over our beliefs in gods, spirits and aliens. I was glad that our tastes in books were similar and we had promised to exchange our Sidney Sheldon collections. Scrolling through his playlist, I had found some artists I had never heard of, but also some that I loved. As expected, he listened to mainstream artists such as Coldplay, Drake and Khalid, but he also had a wide collection of music by Rascal Flatts and Andrew Belle. I even found some R Kelly, which he laughed off as guilty pleasure.

"Oh shoot! Aryan, I have class tomorrow morning and I won't be getting enough sleep tonight!" I said looking into my watch which now said 5 a.m.

"Let me walk you back then, you'll be needing the beauty sleep."

I smacked him and he took my hand, entwining it with his. Hand in hand, I strolled with him, wishing the night didn't have to end.

3

BII had an abundance of assignments and projects, but even when buried under the workload, my thoughts wandered home. Talking to mum and dad on the phone had become a daily routine, but I sometimes felt like I was losing touch with Radhika. All the information I had about her life was from her social media accounts. I realized that I didn't know who her friends were anymore or what she did in her free time. Hell, I didn't even know if she was seeing someone. My phone calls with her had been distant and although she promised to Skype when she had time, I hadn't seen her face since my last visit. I understood that she had to study really hard, but people needed breaks, especially during intense prep. Stressing about this on my own would do no good, so I decided to give her a call.

"Hi Radhika! Where have you been, you bitch? Please save me from this place, I've missed you so much."

"Raina, I'll save you once I get there. That's not going to happen until I study my ass off."

"You're such a nerd. Could you please give me the 411 on your life?"

"The same old. My head has been buried in books since the day you left. You tell me?"

"I was hoping to live off vicariously from you. What interesting things do you expect in Indore? I did meet a guy though, his name is Aryan and—"

"Raina, I'm really busy right now. I'm sorry you'll have to tell me later," Radhika said cutting me off. I was slightly hurt by her sudden dismissal. As a child, she used to beg me to tell her stories about my life.

"Okay fine, can you give the phone to mum?" I mumbled half-heartedly.

After assuring my mother that I was safe and healthy, she unleashed all her soap opera updates on me. I hung up soon after, giving her the same excuse Radhika had given me.

"I have to study, Mum. I'll talk to you tomorrow," I promised.

The truth was, Radhika's behaviour was still gnawing at me. I've always been an overthinker and I knew that this would keep me up at night. Overthinkers focus on small issues until they're big enough to blow up in their heads. Minuscule issues such as a friend acting strange grow into the feeling that they don't want you anymore. That notion sticks in your head until you meet them again and you realize that you wasted hours focusing on something that they probably didn't even notice. It's difficult for an overthinker to get bored, because when you have nothing to keep yourself busy with, then your mind starts running its wheels. It complicates life into shades of grey, but it also makes sure you're prepared for what life may throw at you. After all, you've considered the possibility in your head a hundred times already.

My stomach grumbled, interrupting my train of thought. The three slices of Pepperoni pizza I had had for lunch hadn't been enough to satisfy my appetite and I needed to refuel. I walked downstairs to the tuck shop, planning on buying bars of Snickers and Twix. My pyjamas and hoodie kept me warm against the unforgiving weather. I pulled the white hood over me as I sauntered into the heavy rain avoiding the pellets of water spitting at me. The perpetually rainy weather added to the gloomy atmosphere of IBII. That, along with the lack of bright lights and cheery colours in the institution, advertised the university's brand. Their students were serious professionals, ready to make their mark in the corporate world. They didn't need the almost child-like upliftment of liveliness that I did.

The tuck shop had a long waiting line. Evidently, I wasn't the only one who felt like pigging out during the rainy season, not that it was ever sunny in Indore. I had never really been conscious about my weight except for one summer when I had tried to go to the gym and had failed miserably. On my first day, I had been really enthusiastic and had welcomed the atmosphere of determination and energy. I had observed the manner in which the floors caught the sweat whereas the walls listened to the groans and beats of the music pumping from the speakers. I had tried every machine while I stared into the mirror that controlled the perception of myself. I subsequently bought a membership and all sorts of athletic requirements, including track shoes, a sports bag, tights and multiple sports bras. I went to the gym the next day, but my motivation had dimmed and the floors didn't seem fascinating anymore. Look, you're on the fitter side, so you'll be toned if you come here once or twice a week, and be careful of what you eat, I had reasoned with myself. My trainer had told me about how he encouraged those who made the time, but shunned those who failed to come after their very first day. Alas, his threats couldn't hold up for too long and taunted by the desire to laze in my room, I soon stopped going altogether. Dancing had kept my body in shape in Delhi and I figured that the amount of walking I had to deal with on a daily basis here would balance out the junk food anyway. With a lack of parental supervision came the onset of living on Maggi and chocolates.

I opened my earmarked page of *Hunger Games*, finding peace in the battle. I had read the novel a couple of times before, but I kept going back anyway. The love triangle kept me entrapped and I was thoroughly confused about whether Katniss should choose Peeta or Gale. My choice differed each time I reread the book. Bibliomaniacs often chastise earmarking of books, but even though I didn't desire any wear or tear on the fresh pages, I could never locate a bookmark around me. I looked around, wondering if the tuck shop would have any, but the odds weren't in my favour. Earmarking would have to do until I visited Delhi again. I could probably pick one up from the airport itself, and while I was at it, I would buy a couple of new books. I had been meaning to try out disparate authors and I could already smell the familiar scent of going through the pages of an unopened and inviting novel. That scent combined with the smell of coffee reminded me of all the mornings back at home. If I ever learnt anything about the perfume business, I would definitely try capturing the heady combination in a bottle. That would probably put my MBA degree to good use, since I hadn't yet decided what I wanted to do further in life. I remembered Aryan eagerly asking me what my passion was. I had told him that I danced, but that was more of a hobby than a passion. Aryan hadn't given me the disappointed look I usually got from my relatives, but had reassuringly told me that I'd find my fire in my own time. I preferred that outlook over the general mindset of figuring out your life when you're ten. I didn't understand how I was supposed to decide what I was going to be doing for the rest of my life without trying it first.

"Do you mind if I borrow that book after you're done? I think we're in the same dorm and I just finished what I was reading." The girl standing in front of me said.

She had tanned skin and perfect posture, immediately making her look tall and intimidating. She carried herself with an aura of sophistication that I appreciated.

"Yeah sure, I'm just rereading it. Feel free to take it anytime." I smiled back.

"I totally forgot to introduce myself, I'm so rude. My name is Savera Nanda, but my friends call me Savi. Tell me about yourself."

"I'm Raina Kapoor and I'm from Delhi. This is my first year here."

"I'm in my first year too, but this place has grown on me. I'm used to travelling around. I was born in Mumbai, but I've lived in most of India really. I was in Kolkata before this and my parents are still there right now. Come with me and meet some of the other girls here."

I followed Savera and she introduced me to a group of girls huddled in a corner. I had seen a few of them in the same classes as mine.

"Meet Sanjana, Malaika, Priya, Anjali and Anya. Guys, this is Raina, she rereads *Hunger Games* and she's from Delhi!"

I looked at all their faces, memorising their names. My friends often joked that I should have been the assistant in *The Devil Wears Prada*. Attaching names to faces came naturally to me.

"Hi Sanjana, Malaika, Priya, Anjali and Anya," I repeated after Savi.

"With that memory, I can see what you're doing here," Anya said.

The girls quickly included me in their group and their individual personalities came to me as a surprise. I had expected the people over here to be boring and academics-oriented. These girls seemed like interesting people and I could imagine myself being friends with them. The stereotypes about IBII had clouded my judgment and had stopped me from being open minded about the students around me. Usually an extrovert, I had gone into my own shell and hadn't really interacted with anyone apart from Aryan. I had been missing out by my own fault and I mentally kicked myself for not making more of an effort.

"Thanks, Savi," I said giving her a grateful smile.

4

My days improved immensely once I started making friends with the people around me. I had become increasingly close to Savi and Anya and I found myself at ease with them. My relationship with Aryan had also been progressing at just the right pace. We had now exchanged numbers and we sometimes met up, before and after classes. I enjoyed his company, whether we were sharing notes or getting coffee from the mess. He listened to me like he was absorbing my words and not just waiting to return to another topic of conversation. I had started developing feelings for him and skimming over his little quirks was slowly turning into a habit. I racked my mind over whether he felt the same for me, secretly liking the infatuation that had taken over my brain. It was odd for me to make a connection so fast, but his soft spirit and his quick wit had left me completely enthralled.

I spent a lot of my evenings with the same group of girls I had met at the tuck shop and even they noticed my crimson cheeks when I received a text from him. They had seen us spending time together and Anya encouraged me to drop hints regarding how I felt. I had never been in a situation where I had to pursue a guy and I was completely lost. In the past, I had only developed feelings for someone when their feelings were evident towards me, and I hadn't quite deciphered how to go about the chase.

The delicious nervousness swept over me once again as I began to discuss my action plan with Anya. She was dressed in a pink kurta which highlighted her light eyes and delicate build well.

"Raina, we've all seen the way you guys are around each other. I can tell that you both are into one another just by the sheer amount of sexual tension between you two."

"Please, he has lots of girl friends whom he spends time with, I'm sure."

"Don't you mean admirers? He doesn't give them half the attention he gives you."

The remark sent a chill down my spine. Did Aryan notice me more than other girls?

"Okay, but he hasn't made any indication towards being more than just friends. What do I do?" I groaned.

"Flirt subtly. Compliment him a little. Hold his arm when possible. Let him know you're interested, but leave him wanting more. I'm good at this," she smirked.

"For god's sake Raina, this is the twenty-first century. You can just go up to him and tell him how you feel. We don't need to debate over this," Savi butted in.

"I'll overcome this shyness eventually, but for now, just give me advice," I replied.

"I'll give you even better advice: you have a presentation coming up and I suggest you go study."

Savi was right. I did have to present my research on advertisement and its effects on consumer preferences. The bounds of being in IBII, we were here to get our final installment of education so that we would be employable adults by the end of it and that required a good amount of work. I was technically an adult, but I sure didn't feel like one. My friends and I were always discussing how in a couple of years a few of us may be married and it boggled my mind each time. I couldn't even drink legally in Delhi, so being twenty-two didn't feel like I was given any real responsibility. Although I was old enough to work, vote and go to prison, I wasn't old enough to handle myself if intoxicated. Didn't the government always make so much sense?

I searched for different forms of guerrilla advertisement online and I was fascinated by the creativity behind some of the ads. My personal favourite had to be the flash mobs. It was the perfect way to incorporate society and grab attention and it had a special place in my heart after watching the movie, *Friends with Benefits*. Marketing was an interesting field, but it required an excessive amount of rote learning. So I had come to the conclusion that Finance would be better suited for me. The only drawback to Finance would be getting a desk job. To each his own, but I would never be able to sit in one place for eight hours. A job that required me to get up and get things done had to be infinitely better. Working as a manager who had to hold meetings in exotic locations could be an ideal option, but first, I had to finish this damn research. I typed my notes on the Macbook my parents had gotten me as a surprise. I think Radhika had been a little jealous at first because she still had to use the desktop, but I was sure she would get one when she'd come here.

I was satisfied with the presentation I had come up with. It had taken a couple of hours, but to add a finishing touch, I had decided to design my own advertisement for a shampoo bottle based on what consumers liked to see. I had quickly learnt that bold colours and texts caught the consumers' attention, especially if they were uneducated and didn't have any other criteria for making the decision to buy the bottle. I checked my phone contently and was surprised to see two missed calls from Aryan. I was just about to call him back when his name flashed on my screen again.

Meet me outside in 10

Gee, thanks for the explanatory message Aryan. I changed from my comfortable pyjamas to a pair of white pants and a red top. I had time, so I put some lipstick on and brushed through my hair. He had seen me looking dull and tired after classes, but a little effort never hurt anybody.

I skipped downstairs and saw him standing outside the gate wearing a burgundy v neck t-shirt with beige pants. I could tell how muscular his body was through the tight shirt and I was immediately filled with longing.

"Raina, this is for you!" he said handing me five pink tulips. Like most girls, I absolutely loved flowers, but I had never had a particular favourite. Roses seemed too mainstream and sunflowers too abundant. Tulips were suddenly special in my eyes and they became my newfound favourite.

"I found these in some shady garden at the back of the campus. The rainy weather had torn them from their roots, but they still looked beautiful, so I thought I would get them for you," he said giving me a timid smile.

His smile was also my newfound favourite, I realized. I wrapped my arms around his waist and hugged him. He was too tall for me to reach his shoulders, but I liked it that way. He hugged my shoulders back, making me feel warm and protected.

"I love them, Aru," I said grinning.

He laughed and said that he liked being called Aru. Warmth filled up my heart again.

"Well, it was Aru or Malik. You can take your pick."

"Any name is fine as long as you're the one calling me, Raina."

I rolled my eyes at this remark and asked him what he was doing in a shady garden by himself.

"Who said I was by myself? I was walking with Aditi after class and we happened to stumble across that garden."

I felt a sharp pang of jealousy, taking me by surprise. Was I really this smitten over a person I had met a month back? And what was with the jealousy? I had definitely never been the type to be possessive before and Aryan wasn't even mine to be possessive about. We weren't together, but he did bring me flowers on his walk with Aditi, and that had to count for something.

"What's bothering you, Raina?" he said looking confused.

"I was just thinking about my presentation tomorrow," I lied guiltily.

"Tell me about it," he said earnestly, making me want to hug him even more.

5

December: First Year of IBII

Aryan and I had started behaving like we were in a full-fledged relationship. We spent most of our time with each other and when we had prior commitments, we were constantly updating each other through Snapchat and WhatsApp. I had gotten used to waking up to a flood of notifications from him tagging me on random dog videos and funny puns. The other night, we had stayed up late drinking coffee, and he had called me his best friend. I know I was supposed to feel good about my new position in his life, but that would be a reasonable explanation as to why we acted like we were dating. We were best friends, that's all. We didn't have to be attracted to each other to spend all our time together.

Today we had the night off, which was rare in our hectic schedule. Although we were allowed to venture outside campus until 11 p.m., there was always some assignment or test the following day that restricted us. The first year of the MBA here was supposed to be way tougher than the second, in which we could opt for an exchange programme for a semester abroad. I had heard that in our year, the semester would be in France and I was looking forward to the experience eagerly. To be selected for the programme, I had to make sure I had a good rank in my batch. This year, I had been sailing in the thirties, but in the next year, I would have to get to the top fifteen. It wouldn't be too tough considering they almost halved the required credits in the second year.

Aryan had told me to get dressed by 6 p.m. for a surprise. It was 5 p.m. and I looked over my wardrobe finding an appropriate outfit. When I came here from Delhi, I had innocently carried my best tops and bodycon dresses, but I had never really found an occasion to wear them. Tonight, I decided to wear a floral dress with a denim jacket and white shoes. The outfit was casual, but it made me look great. I sprayed some perfume on my neck and left my dorm room excitedly.

"What is this surprise you have in store for me, Malik?"

"Have you seen yourself in the mirror, Raina? Look at you! You look absolutely ravishing," he exclaimed with his mouth open.

Delighted to have this effect on him, I gave him a little twirl, knowing my dress was revealing my toned thighs.

"As for the surprise, you'll have to wait and watch. My lips are sealed."

"Give me a hint," I pouted.

He took my hand in his and we walked to an entrance where a cab was waiting for us. I was usually good with routes, but I had no idea about the whereabouts of Indore outside campus. Aryan had already put the drop location on his phone and the Uber driver drove us to the secret place quietly. I noticed that Aryan had still not let go of my hand.

"Close your eyes, Raina. We have some walking to do."

"Don't we always?"

We had stopped in the middle of nowhere and I wondered if I should be scared to be in a deserted area in the dark. My parents' warnings came back to me, but Aryan made me feel safe in a way I couldn't explain.

"Close your eyes, baba."

"How do I know that you're not planning on kidnapping me, Malik?" I teased him.

"I wouldn't have to pay for a cab if that was what I wanted to do. I would have plenty opportunities back on campus, weakling. Now close your eyes and promise you won't open them until I say so."

I closed my eyes and he guided me through the swampy road for the next five minutes. I patiently waited for him to tell me when I could see where he was taking me. He had really built up the whole surprise thing, but I didn't think there was much to do in the city. After walking for a few more minutes, I could smell the distinct scent of food being fried in vats of oil. Upon further inspection, I realized that I could also hear the faint sound of music.

"Guess where we are!"

I listened harder, observing the sounds of clinking change and chugging machinery.

"I don't know, Aru. Are we crashing a wedding?"

"Open your eyes," he said laughing excitedly.

I tried to look around as the blinding lights caused me to blink profusely.

"What? I don't understand?"

"Take a step back and look where we are. It's a travelling fair! I don't know why it's here at this point of time, but I looked for events in Indore and found this. It's slightly like the melas that are organized in Kolkata during Durga Puja. It's only here for five days and today is the fourth, which is supposed to be the least crowded. I guess the novelty wears off after the first few days, but the last day everyone shows up once again to bid adieu to it for another year."

"Aru, you don't know how much I love roller coasters. Let's do this!" I said inhaling the smell of the popcorn in the air.

"A girl of my own heart." Aryan smiled.

We started with the unthreatening rides like the carousel and then moved up to larger rides such as the Ferris wheel. As we reached the top, the roar of the fair dimmed and I kicked my feet out at the open air, enjoying the moment. Sneaking a peek at Aryan, I was glad to see that he looked as happy as I felt.

"You can hold my hand if you're scared."

"Please."

"Hold my hand anyway."

In an hour's time, we were done with all the rides and we stopped at a candy floss counter.

"The blue one for her and the pink one for me," he said to the operator.

"Don't assume the colour of my candy based on my gender," I said acting offended.

"It's good you clarified that now, I was going to win you a toy car next."

He went up to one of the many game stalls which hung stuffed toys as bait for playing the game. This stall contained a set of darts and the person who hit the center three times in a row would get to take the stuffed animal home. Aryan tried to hit the centre, but ended up only touching the border once, out of his five chances.

"I should probably tell you, I haven't played darts before."

"Really? I couldn't tell," I smirked "Let me do it."

I had played darts at a sports bar twice before and I hoped that I would get the centre. I ended up hitting the border three times, but I had no luck touching the taunting red circle.

"Let's just move on before we embarrass ourselves further."

The next game required hitting a tall stack of cans with a ball. If all the cans fell, then the winner would get a teddy bear which was half the size of a person. I went first, but it was harder than I expected, and I had four cans still standing in the bottom-most row. Aryan tried after me and managed to hit all the cans with one ball, beaming at the stall like it had been created for him.

"I like the prizes of this stall more anyway," he said while the owner stretched to get the bear off the rack. We strolled away from the stall and I looked at the stars above us that were almost never visible amidst the polluted Delhi skies. I noticed that we were reaching an isolated area and the distance between us was consistently reducing.

"This is for you. A bear for my human," he said gazing into my eyes with an intensity I hadn't seen before. The tension between us rose and he grabbed my face and pulled it towards his. I glanced at his lips and suddenly we were kissing one another frantically. My arms flew around his neck and he held my waist, discovering my mouth with his tongue. His fingers ran down my spine, causing my back to arch and I kissed him as deeply as I could. He tasted better than I could have ever imagined and I immediately knew that this was what I had been waiting for.

I felt like I could have stayed in his arms for a lifetime, but our curfew had to be met. We reluctantly called an Uber to go back to campus. I rested my head on his shoulder the entire ride back, blissful in our bubble.

"Raina, wake up!" Aryan nudged me awake.

I looked around groggily as the IBII board outside the institute glared at me.

"We've reached, babe."

Babe. This was new. I had often cringed at couples with cheesy nicknames, but this lit my heart on fire.

"Would you like me to drop you to your room?" he asked me and I realized that he was hoping I would say no.

"Do I have any other alternatives?"

"Yeah, you could always walk back alone," he joked.

"Fine, bye!" I said dramatically, beginning to walk away, when he grabbed my wrist and pulled me back.

"Your other alternative is that you get to spend the night at mi casa. That means my house, you know. In actuality, my room."

A girl spending the night in a guy's room was frowned upon, but it was a hell of a lot better than a guy spending the night in the girl's room, which was completely against the rules. I had no inclination towards being around the other men and I had heard that the bathrooms in their dorm were practically unusable, but I was curious to see Aryan's room. I had never actually been there before as most of our visits had been confined to the mess or the gardens. I would also get to stay with him for another ten hours. All my clothes were still in my room and I did want to change out of my dress now. Weighing my options, I realized that there were no real options to weigh. One of the most important rules in any country that holds a democratic election is that it has to give its citizens at least two disparate and worthy choices. If you're being given parties that are referred to by different names but follow the same ideology, you're not really giving the citizens a fair array to choose from. Similarly, if the only other party that is allowed to contest is ridiculously behind the first party, then again, it just *seems* like the citizen has a choice, when practically, he or she doesn't. For me, the second case applied; I didn't have two worthy choices. The comforts of my room didn't stand a chance against Aryan.

"Yes, I've heard of the phrase, Aru. Looks like I'll be having a change of scenery tonight."

"That's exactly what I wanted to hear," he said grabbing me in the process and pulling me onto his back.

"You're tired, so you get a piggy back ride."

I jumped landing on his back and he ran to his room bouncing me along as if I weighed nothing. I giggled with joy, but I soon became nervous as a dark thought snuck in my head. Appropriate societal behaviour had just struck me and I wasn't sure if agreeing to spend the night insinuated sex. I knew I wasn't ready to take that leap yet.

We reached his room and he collapsed on his bed. I took in his room slowly. He had the same essential furniture as me, but his room was smaller. It was also painted with a drab yellow colour that made it a lot duller than my white room. Apart from a few clothes lying astray, his room was pristine. I could never be bothered with cleaning my room like he did, and it was evident by the way his clothes lay folded neatly. If he had been sleeping in my room, we would have had to spend a considerable amount of time making it spacious enough for two people, starting with the books sprawled on my bed. When mum lectured me about my room, I often replied saying that life was messy, which was just my excuse for being too lazy to change my ways.

"Welcome to my room."

"It's a good thing you live on the ground floor. Your back was about to give out," I said referring to his collapsed figure on the bed.

"Please, I could have carried you up ten flights of stairs," he said haughtily.

"I wouldn't take your word for it."

"Take my tongue instead."

A wave of arousal ran through my spine at his words. How could he manage to be sexy at all times?

He beckoned me towards his bed and I sat on his lap, pressing my lips against his. The tension between us immediately amplified and he took charge, laying me down carefully, all the while not stopping to take a breath. My hands grabbed his back and I felt his hands go up my waist. I didn't want to stop him, but I knew I had to. It was too soon for this and we hadn't even spoken about commitment. I wanted him, but I strengthened my resolve against it.

"Aryan, not yet. I'm not ready to go further than this right now."

"I'm so sorry! I should have asked," he said planting a kiss on my forehead.

I was impressed at the way he handled it and I pushed my tongue back into his mouth.

I felt Aryan's breath near my neck while he bit me gently. This would leave a mark tomorrow, but I didn't care. I wanted to give him my body, but the voice in my head acted as a barrier. I needed to talk to him about my past and all my insecurities.

"Listen, let's stop for a while. I have to tell you something."

Aryan stiffened visibly and he now had a solemn look on his face.

"I recently dated someone, but I never told you about him before. I guess talking about him meant admitting my insecurities to you and I wanted you to see me in the best light. I want you to understand why I'm stopping myself from going further, even though I think we both want this."

I looked at Aryan's face and he urged me to continue with a concerned look in his eyes.

"His name is Akshat and we dated for six months. I know that's not a long time and we weren't in love, but we did like each other a whole lot. We had covered three bases in four months' time and he kept asking me to make love to him. I had just decided that I would lose my virginity to him, but then something happened that changed everything. I thought that things were going well between us until one night when we went to a night club with a couple of our friends. We were ordering drinks at the bar when a sultry girl showed up wearing a short dress that showed off her tiny waist and large cleavage. She was the type of girl that people noticed, and not only because of her outfit, but also because of her confidence. She acted as if she recognised Akshat, although she wasn't in either of our friend circles. She hugged him familiarly and I saw a panicked expression on Akshat's face. She continued to whisper something about bathroom sex while he tried to move away. Akshat and I had both been virgins when we met and I immediately realized what had happened between the both of them. I was shocked and humiliated and I ran from the club, not caring that I didn't have a ride back home. He ran after me, apologising profusely, and I pushed him away asking him to leave me alone. I took a cab home even though I wasn't allowed to travel in cabs once it was dark out. One look at my face and my mum didn't ask any questions when I got back. I told her to leave me alone and I just went to my room and cried my eyes out. The image of them kissing and doing what not kept flooding my mind and it was absolutely horrible. It hurt me immensely, Aryan, and I still shudder at the memory. My ego took a huge blow along with my feelings. The next day, Akshat sent me a long message on how he had met her at a party when he was tipsy, and she had seduced him into bed. They had had sex, but he said it meant nothing to him. He had just done it because he apparently couldn't say no to the offer, and because I wouldn't give him the same. He said he loved me and he would do anything to make it up to me. Those words didn't matter to me. He sent flowers to my house and showed up at my doorstep twice. I never contacted him after that night, and in a few weeks' time, he stopped trying to call as well. I have a huge vendetta against cheaters. The thought of him touching another girl while I was probably sitting at home and missing him disgusted me to another level. That whole relationship left me with some trust issues and I decided to not go too far physically unless I was completely in love. I know this is a tough thing to hear, and in this generation, being a virgin at twenty-two is odd, and if this changes anything between us, then I'll understand," I said while I tried to wipe away the tears that had started pooling up in my eyes.

"Raina, look at me."

He held my face up while I worriedly wiped away the remnants of my tears.

"You are beautiful. I have not had the balls to say this to you yet, but you are. I don't know Akshat, but I can already tell you that any guy who cheats on a girl, let alone on someone like you, is an asshole. What he did should show you how messed up his priorities are. Not all guys are going to be like that and I definitely am not. As for the part about this changing anything between us, you mustn't be as smart as I thought you were previously. Something as trivial as this couldn't make me move an inch away from you. I completely understand why you'll take time to trust me and I'll give you that time. You get my time because you're my priority. If I haven't made it clear enough, I've developed serious feelings for you and I want you to be my girlfriend."

"Yes!"

"Yes?"

"Yes."

Delhi wasn't home anymore, he was.

6

August: Second Year of IBII

I walked towards the academics block hoping to see Aryan on the way. I knew he had an extra class at 1:45 p.m. and would have probably left his room by now. All our courses were technically over, but some students had taken advanced classes ten days before the semester started to get ahead in the next year. Aryan was one of them and I had promised him that even I would give them a try. The pressure of obtaining placements would be upon us when these classes were actually supposed to take place. Most of the students would be working hard to ensure their selection in top companies at that time and wouldn't have time to focus on these classes.

I had told Aryan that I would be reaching Indore the day after and I paced towards the academics block, excited to surprise him. I couldn't wait to see the look on his face when he saw me. We had been together since more than nine months now, and yet it felt like we were still in the honeymoon phase where every small separation felt like we had been away for weeks. This particular separation had been especially difficult as I had been in Delhi for a month, whilst Aryan was stuck here. Used to living together, it had been strange waking up without him next to me. All of us had gotten a break after our first-year examinations in June, but he hadn't been able to visit his family because his parents had been unaware of the dates and had already booked tickets to New York for a vacation. It had been too late for him to get his visa, and he hadn't had many other options left. He had to return to campus before our second year officially began.

My trip to Delhi had been more work-related than anything else. As soon as my exams had finished, I was called back to become Radhika's personal tutor. I didn't mind doing it since the end result was Radhika in IBII, but we were sisters, and like all sisters, we got on each other's nerves. Teaching her was always a task, since we both did things so differently. Her mind was more on the creative side, and I didn't think her aptitude matched the mathematics part of the exam. But all that said, I knew that her hard work had to make up for it. I would get annoyed every time she couldn't solve a question that was seemingly simple to me. I had to explain the same solution to her again and again, even though it felt logical to me. She would then get annoyed at not being able to do the questions I could with ease. This cycle continued until we desperately needed a break from the preparation. We would then curl up with some of the silly Bollywood movies we watched as kids and caramel ice cream which we both loved. It was amusing to see what we had liked in the past and we couldn't comprehend how these movies could have possibly been our favourites at one point of time. They were extremely dramatic and sometimes completely illogical. There was also an abundance of random songs and dances. We would laugh at the theatrics and then cry at the emotions. The next day, I would start teaching her in the morning and the day would play out exactly like the previous one. I did find time to meet some of my college and school friends and I was relieved to find that nothing had changed between us. I had been terrified that it might be awkward meeting them after so long, but we were already updated on each other's lives through our group chats on WhatsApp. So once we met each other, we quickly fell into the rhythm of being around one another. Charvi, my best friend from school, was in medical college, whereas Mahima, my closest friend from college, was still studying Economics.

One time, we were sleeping over at Charvi's for the night and had just come to her room after a huge meal consisting of delights such as shawarma and butter chicken, two of my favourite foods. We all lay in bed discussing the stressful elements of our lives and laughed at each other's silly antics which we had forgotten about. I was happy that Mahima was still in a healthy relationship with her high school boyfriend, Raj. It had been six years now and they were still perfectly content. I wondered if Aryan and I would be able to go so far. I had blind faith in us, which was dangerous for me in case he messed up, but I figured that trust was the most important element of any successful relationship and it was okay for me to believe in him so passionately. I didn't quite know where I would be in the future, but I believed that we would make it anyway. Nobody had made me feel like this before and I welcomed the newness of it all. Raj called Mahima twice during our sleepover and both times her tough exterior softened visibly. I couldn't hear his responses, but she giggled and blushed at the things he said and I couldn't help but wonder if I looked like that while talking to Aryan.

I scanned the campus, still unable to spot him. Unlike most rainy days in Indore, the day was hot and humid. My palazzos began to cling to my legs and I hurried towards the entrance of the block. I didn't like being away from Aryan, but I sure as hell didn't mind being away from the musty buildings of IBII that cried for a paint job. The campus could have been beautiful if anyone had cared about the infrastructure. It needed a renovation terribly, but I knew that our low tuition fee would not be able to cover the expenditure. We were charged a tenth of what students abroad were, in order to give deserving students access to quality education even if they couldn't afford many other resources. I had to hold grudging respect for the socialist philosophy even though it meant that IBII had no funds for necessities that were proclaimed luxuries.

A figure in white caught my eye, taking me away from my thoughts. Aryan strolled lazily, wearing a white muscle T-shirt and grey jogging tracks that hung around his waist in a way that made me swoon. I noticed something, or rather someone, hanging around him as well. I tried to stifle my annoyance at the sight of Aditi gazing at him in a way that made me feel sick. Aryan said they were friends, but it was obvious that she had the hots for him. I couldn't blame her for that, but I could blame her for her shameless attempts to catch his attention, even though she was well aware that he had a girlfriend. He helped me feel really secure in what we had, but girls like Aditi pissed me off. Anya told me that she had heard Aditi boasting about the number of guys who had cheated on their girlfriends because of her in the laundry room. I understood that she had no responsibility towards those girlfriends to not hook up with their men, but it seemed like a nasty thing to do either way. I would hate to be in a position where a girl was getting her heart broken due to a hook up that I didn't really care for. I had asked Aryan later why he would even want to be friends with someone like her, but his response had been that he didn't care much as long as she kept that part of her life away from him.

I put away my thoughts of Aditi and smiled at the sight of Aryan, a few steps away from me. "Aru!" I tried to take his attention away from her. He looked towards me with an expression I wish I could have captured on camera. His wide grin reached his lit up eyes as he started towards me. Aditi, on the other hand, looked at me grudgingly.

"Raina, you're here! You said you were coming tomorrow, you cheeky thing. I'm so glad you're here," he said sweeping me into his arms. He planted a kiss on my forehead and picked me up, swirling me around. Public display of affection was technically not allowed inside the university and my rule abiding ass would have usually winced, but I didn't seem to care anymore. From the corner of my eye, I noticed Aditi slithering into the building with a look of dejection on her face. It seemed to make the moment even sweeter and I buried my face in his neck.

"I missed you, babe," he whispered in my ear.

"More Aru, always more," I said hugging him fiercely.

Aryan left for his class, already fifteen minutes late, and I walked to the men's dorm, ready to take a nap. I was glad to be out of the blistering heat and into the air conditioned rooms. I thanked the gods that this was one luxury IBII granted us. Amidst the heat of India, I believed that it was almost a requirement, especially when we needed to focus on our books. I looked around the organized room with familiarity and opened the cupboard to take a blanket out. No matter how hot it was outside, I needed a blanket to cover me up while I slept. It gave me an odd sense of protection and was absolutely necessary for me to get any sleep. The room looked just how I had left it, with everything in its own place. I snuggled into the bed which smelt like the beachy scent of Aryan's aqua cologne. I had moved into his room in the early days of our relationship, willing to sacrifice my cheery room for his dull one. He was all the cheer I needed and he wasn't allowed in the girls' dorm. The room was big enough for the both of us and I easily found space in his neat wardrobes. We went to sleep together every night and I enjoyed the comfortable routine immensely. His friends, Piyush and Aman, had also learnt to knock before entering. I had become well acquainted with them and enjoyed their mindless banter about the latest consoles and games.

The flight from Delhi to Indore was only eighty minutes, but I was still exhausted. I switched positions on the bed, trying to find one that was comfortable. I turned left and right, but something tugged at my stomach throughout. Was I forgetting something? I checked my phone wondering what I could be missing. I had a habit of putting in all the important event reminders on the notes application. I scoured over all the dates I had noted. What was the date today? I checked my calendar, appreciating how efficient my smartphone was. The 10th of August. Crap, it was the day Radhika's results were to be out!

I called her anxiously, listening to the ringing on the other line. No answer.

I called her one more time and then two more times after. What was happening? Had she gone out to celebrate? Didn't she want to tell her sister about the news?

I called her again, determined to get through to her. On the final ring, I heard a click on the other side.

"How was it?" I gushed.

"I didn't get through."

7

"That's not possible" I replied to Radhika in shock. I had always just assumed that she would be coming here, without a shadow of doubt.

"Apparently they had better candidates. I'm sure you're happy though," she replied, her voice bitter.

"Me? Why would I be happy? I worked so hard to make sure you get here."

"Please. You just relished in the satisfaction you got from being able to act like the smart one. You never really wanted me there."

"All I've wanted was for you to be here with me."

"Don't bother lying now. You get to be the star child, as usual."

I could almost feel her rolling her eyes at me.

"What's really bothering you?"

"You're always the one under the spotlight. Since we've been kids!"

"What do you mean, Radhika?"

"All I've ever heard is, 'Why can't you be more like your perfect sister? She's so smart. She's definitely going to make it big some day.' What about me? Nobody believes in me. Even after giving the exam, the first thing that was said to me was that it was okay if I don't get in because I have options abroad. Dad didn't even ask me how it went. Everyone just assumed that I would probably not get in, even though I studied twice as hard as you."

"I believed in you. I believed that you would get through."

"No. You're always trying to play yourself off as the saint. It's all your fault. If you hadn't constantly been under the limelight, maybe I would have been given some importance too."

The realisation dawned on me that this wasn't about her getting into IBII at all. She had harboured these feelings for a long time and had finally gained the courage to unleash them.

"What can I do, Radhs? I'm sorry you feel this way."

"Get out of my life. I'll go to the States now. To some university that's probably better than IBII, but it still won't be good enough in our parents' eyes. It should be easy for you to back the fuck off then."

I blinked away tears at what Radhika was saying to me. When had she even begun to hate me?

"Maybe then I'll finally be able to live my life the way I want to, instead of constantly being haunted by your shadow," she continued.

"I'm your sister, Radhika."

"I wish you never existed."

The words were like a slap across my face. The sister I loved so much, didn't want me around her.

"You really don't want to talk to me? Ever again?"

"Yes," she said slamming down the line, reminding me of how she used to slam the door when we fought as kids. This didn't feel the same though. This felt horribly wrong. We said words we didn't mean all the time, but even our worst fights had never gotten so out of hand. I wiped a tear away as I heard Aryan enter his room.

"Raina? What happened?"

I sobbed through the story as he held me, rocking me patiently.

"Sisters fight. You've told me that the both of you fought a lot. This is just another one of those fights. You'll make up in no time."

"This wasn't like that. It wasn't in the heat of the moment. She's been feeling this way for a long time. She really doesn't want me around," I cried to him.

"It's impossible not to want you around," he said.

I knew he was trying to make me feel better and I flashed him a grateful smile. My mind was still unravelling why my sister held so much resentment towards me. I searched for any sort of justification for not noticing her feelings before. Trying to absolve myself from blame, I desperately grasped for theories that didn't make it my fault. I thought of a vague and distant memory of my mother complaining about Radhika always blaming others for her own faults. I guess she had been doing the same with me for a longer time than anyone knew.

"Go to bed. She'll be fine tomorrow," Aryan coaxed me.

I nodded, curling myself up in his arms.

Soon enough, I drifted off to a place where there were no problems.

8

"**B**ook the 5 p.m. flight, I'm leaving right away!" I heard Aryan shout into the phone, waking me from my peaceful haven. I had been having a lovely dream about being immensely successful and sitting at a fancy restaurant enjoying delicious food. I had just been about to dig into my prawn tempura when his booming voice transported me back to reality. I was vaguely annoyed at being woken up in this abrupt manner and I tried to piece his words together in my half asleep state.

"No, it's not fine. I want the earliest flight available."

"Yes, my bags are packed already."

"Take care of her, I'll be there soon."

I looked around our room and spotted his blue suitcase on the floor. He had thrown in a couple of clothes in a haphazard manner. This wasn't like him. Aryan was going somewhere and he was in a hurry.

"Where are you going, Malik?"

"My mother is in the hospital. They won't tell me why, but I know it's serious. I have a bad feeling about this. If something happens to her, I don't even know—"

His voice started breaking up and I noticed that he was on the verge of tears. I jumped out of bed and held him in my arms, hoping it would be some sort of consolation. I rubbed his back and whispered in his ear, "I know it's going to be fine, Aru. You go and see her. I'll keep tabs on all your classes for you. Have you booked a cab?"

"No, could you please? Raina, I hope to god she's alright, she has to be," he murmured incoherently.

"Yes, the cab is on its way. You have to be strong. For her and for yourself. For me. Take care of everything, I'm sure you're thinking too much of this. It was probably nothing."

I helped him throw in more of his stuff, knowing that if it were serious, he would be needing more of his things than he was thinking about right now. To think that I had just gotten back and he would be going so soon. My phone flashed letting me know that my cab had arrived. IBII was in one of the desolate areas of Indore and the cab service was usually terrible. The estimated wait time was constantly twenty minutes, but today, it had miraculously arrived in five. It was now 3 p.m. and the campus was a good hour-and-a-half away from the airport. He would reach in time only if he hurried.

"Your cab is here, Aru. Please don't worry yourself further and come back to me as soon as you can. I'll miss you."

He kissed me on my lips swiftly and left, leaving the room as empty as I felt.

I had never met his mother, but I had heard a hundred stories about her from Aryan. It was evident that he was the closest to her in his family and that he adored her. Worry flooded through me and I tried to imagine how he must be feeling. I had never lost anyone close to me and had only heard stories about distant relatives passing away. Never having known them, it hadn't mattered to me too much. I hoped aunty would make it through whatever had happened, for her sake and for Aryan's.

Finding his room too upsetting without him, I trudged back to my dorm, still anxious. I had been thinking about her condition since the afternoon and had received no updates from Aryan. I had tried texting him several times but had received no useful responses.

Have you reached?

Yes.

Is everything okay with aunty? What happened? Take care and be strong.

I'm really worried, please let me know soon.

It'll all be better, I promise. Keep faith.

Miss you. Give your family my best wishes.

After the fourth unanswered message, I kept my phone away. I knew that he had a lot going on and he couldn't check his phone continuously, so there was no point in me disturbing him. I decided to call him once before sleeping to make sure he was alright, but until then, I needed some distraction. I was going crazy sitting in my room and coming up with stories of what may have happened and whether she would really be okay like I had assured him. It had already been four hours and I needed to get away.

I walked up the stairs to get to the second floor where Savi's room was, knowing that she had come to campus early as well.

"What happened to you?" Savi asked as soon as I entered.

"Nothing, let's just not talk about it."

"Fine, where's Prince Charming?"

"Savi," I faltered.

"I'm your friend, you can confide in me, you know. Trouble in paradise?"

"Yes, I guess. Not in that way though. Things between us are fine, but he just went back home after receiving a call about his mother. She's in the hospital and I think something serious happened to her. I've been so worried and I need to be there for him. The problem is that I just don't know how to. He hasn't even answered my texts and I know he's going through something difficult, but I just wish I could be of some help."

"Breathe, Raina, breathe. Don't be so upset. What's the point in you taking stress? You're overreacting about this, it'll all be alright."

She was giving me the same advice I had given Aryan and I realized how hollow it sounded.

"You don't know that it'll be alright. Just because you tell me not to take stress or be sad doesn't mean that I'll stop. It's not that easy, I don't have a sad button in my system that I can just turn off."

Savi chewed her lower lip, an indication that she was nervous.

"Look, what I can tell you is that he's probably spending time with her right now after their scare, which is why he can't get back to you. In the meantime, we should do something to take your mind off it. We're always talking about going swimming, but we never do, right? Why not go today?"

"Isn't it a little late for that? It's already dark outside."

"So? Will someone kidnap fragile little Raina in the dark? Don't be such a wuss. Trust me, you'll feel better."

I conceded without giving her much of a fight. Savi and I usually argued quickly and I was always ready with my set of retorts, but right now, I didn't have the energy. Savi looked surprised but smug at my surrender.

"Go, get your costume. I'll meet you at the pool in ten."

I did as I was told and went to my room to take out my red swimsuit. It was modest, but it fit well. I threw on a loose t-shirt and shorts on top and made my way downstairs hoping that this would take my mind off Aryan's mother. Right on time, Savi was waiting for me in front of the pool. I noticed that she was wearing an oversized t-shirt over her costume as well.

"It's silly but I'm excited. I used to swim all the time back in Kolkata and it's been too long. We should have been taking advantage of this pool all along."

I looked around and realized that she was right. The pool was huge and was shaped like the letter 'S'. It was also clean and beautiful. The turquoise hue was startling against the grey of the granite that surrounded it. The pool area had been the newest and only investment made by IBII after its opening and appeared to be the single modern facility amidst the cracking paint and creaking doors. There was also a fountain nearby, making it look like we had entered our very own mystical oasis. I took my t-shirt off and kept it on one of the yellow deck chairs which was yet another surprise. With the fountain, the deck chairs and the pool, I suddenly felt like I wasn't in the dreary IBII, but in a decent hotel. The blue of the water invited me to indulge in it and I left my phone on the chair, eager to check whether the pool was warm or cold.

I won't be able to check my phone once I'm inside, the thought struck me, making me stop dead in my tracks. I looked back and gave the screen a longing look, but I could only see my reflection back. No messages or calls from him yet.

Savi noticed and looked at me sympathetically, "It's okay, you need a break. Leave it, we're not going to be here for more than an hour and there's not anything monumental that you can do in this time anyway. Just relax and join me."

She smiled reassuringly from the water and then splashed water at me when I looked back hesitantly.

I ran back to the deck chair and put my phone on loud, just in case there was any news from him. Clearing my head, I jumped into the pool butt first. I had wrapped my arms around my knees, squatted and jumped. It was a position I had learnt when I visited Germany and it was called the 'Arschbombe' which literally translated to Ass-Bomb. The name was vulgar, but I found the position to be more effective than the classic diving position which hurt once the water hit my body.

Once I was in the water, I gave my body some time to adjust to the cool water instead of the heat that I had been hoping for. Savi had already begun swimming and I shoved my head under water to get used to the cold. The pool wasn't too deep where I was standing and I continued doing so until Savi got back.

"Savi, you're wearing a bikini?" I asked her in shock. I had been too busy enraptured by my surroundings and my thoughts of Aryan to notice her clothing before the translucent and clear water gave it away. She was dressed in a scanty pink bikini and I noticed that even though she didn't show it often, she had a fit physique.

I had nothing against bikinis and I wore them often when I was travelling, but I had left mine in Delhi knowing that the crowd in IBII would consider the outfit inappropriate. I didn't appreciate unwanted leering and was more comfortable in my swimsuit, even though we were surrounded by buildings and not fellow students. The swimming pool was simply too far to attract a crowd and I welcomed the peace of it.

"Why are you surprised?"

"You usually don't show too much skin and also, you know how the people are here."

"You're right, I don't. I choose comfort over beauty and I find my comfort in shirts and sweats instead of halter tops and tight jeans. On the other hand, bikinis are lighter and they help me manoeuvre faster in the water. They're the practical choice, really. As for the people, I don't believe in the over-sexualisation of the female body by society. If they want to stare or call me a slut for my clothing, let them. It shows how narrow-minded and backward they are. Guys can roam around shirtless but crop tops are a big deal here. I'm tired of the patriarchy and I'm going to live as per what's most suitable for me."

She finished her rant and went ahead to swim another lap, leaving me staring back at her in awe. I had never heard Savi talk about feminism before and it was an issue I deeply believed in. People often perceived feminists to be vengeful men hating women, but that was far from true. I believed that a person could either be feminist or a sexist. There was no other way about it. I had never given a thought to my clothes, choosing to cover up in order to avoid being ogled by strange men and even judgmental women. When Savi put it that way, I could see how I had to constantly inconvenience myself because of the mindsets of others. My parents themselves had made remarks forcing me to change my outfits.

"Don't wear that beta, it's night time and it's not safe outside," they had said as if decent clothing could guarantee my safety.

I hadn't questioned them too much and had simply changed. Realising the unfairness of it all, I suddenly felt outraged. I didn't want to perpetuate rape culture by drawing a connection between the clothes women chose to wear and the actions performed by rapists, when I fully knew that their decision had nothing to do with the woman's outfit. Even children got raped for crying out loud, so why were clothes to blame? Our society needed to learn that by making a connection between clothes and those actions, they were insinuating that the women were somehow to be blamed and could have avoided what had happened to them, even though the ones to be blamed should have been the rapists and the rapists alone. Women needed to take Savi as an inspiration and live fearlessly, proud of their bodies and their minds.

As Savi finished her lap, I shared my feelings of awe with her. She smiled at me and promised to finish the conversation in one of our rooms. She wanted to swim and she urged me to do so as well, considering I hadn't moved from my spot since I had entered. I dipped my head under water again, feeling refreshed and level headed. Savi was faster than I realized and my competitive nature forced me to swim more swiftly to catch up with her. I put in all my energy and strength, channelling my frustration so that I could at least come toe to head level with her. She was still way ahead of me and I learnt another fact about her. Savera Nanda was an astounding athlete once she was inside water.

We climbed out of the pool using the silver railings set on both sides of the area. I was dripping all over the place but I couldn't be bothered enough about it. I rushed to check my phone even before fetching a towel. I pressed the centre button on my phone, hoping to see anything from Aryan. My wallpaper, a picture of me with all my friends at a dinner, shone back at me. There were no messages or missed calls obscuring the screen and I put my phone, which was now glistening with the droplets from my hair, back onto the deck chair.

"Still nothing?"

"Radio silence. This really did take my mind off things though, thank you. Also, you're an amazing swimmer."

"Are you flirting with me because your boyfriend is away?", she joked.

"I'm straight. For now," I winked at Savi, causing her to laugh at me.

There were no showers around our little oasis and we walked back to our dorms, exhausted from the day's events. Once I was done with cleaning myself and was snug under my covers, I called Aryan. It was of no avail and I wondered what he would be doing at this very moment. Worried for his mental health, I recited a silent prayer for the safety and well-being of his family.

In the morning when I woke up, amongst all the messages on my phone, there was one that stood out.

She's gone.

9

November: Second Year of IBII

Three months had passed since Aryan's mother passed away and he was still wrecked with misery. He had turned into a walking zombie and refused to display any emotion towards the happenings around him. The experience had transformed him into a hard and cold person and it didn't seem like there was any way to fix it. I felt like I was in serious danger of losing one of the most important people in my life if I hadn't lost him already. I knew that he was in a great deal of suffering, but I couldn't help when he wasn't willing to talk to me. He still followed his daily routine of eating, attending classes and relaxing in the evening, but the energy that I loved about him had disappeared. I had started feeling alone even when he was around and my attempts to reach out to him were always brushed off politely.

After I received the news, I had flown out to Delhi to attend her funeral, but I had been informed that women weren't allowed to go for the cremation. Although I had wanted to hold him until it became better, I knew that it may have been considered inappropriate amongst family and so I had only stood by him, squeezing his arm whenever he looked like he needed some support. It hadn't seemed to be of much help as he had flinched every time I got too close to him. His father had responded to me in the opposite manner, welcoming any words of consolation and thanking me for flying out to be with Aryan. I had also met all of Aryan's relatives which would have been a huge step had it not taken place under such a misfortunate situation. His relatives had been kind to me too and had treated me as if I were family. Aryan seemed to be the only person who hadn't quite wanted me there.

I was trying to be as understanding as I could be, but I had been shut off for way too long. I was just trying to be there for him, but he wasn't letting me in. What made things even worse was my situation with Radhika. I had heard that she had chosen to go to Carla, a reputed university in California. She would be leaving soon, but she hadn't even informed me about her decision, let alone reach out to me. She would be across the world and away from me. Exactly what she had wanted. After the funeral, I had gone back home, devastated about the death. I had imagined meeting his parents numerous times, but now it would never happen. My parents had tried their level best to cheer me up, but Radhika had stuck to her word, confining herself to her room throughout my visit. My ego didn't allow me to knock on her door either. She would talk to me when she really wanted to. In the meantime, I had Aryan to take care of.

I walked to class and hoped that I wouldn't run into him on my way. I felt a stab of guilt course through me, but I couldn't take the small talk anymore. I needed him to tease me lovingly, and more importantly, talk to me about what was going on in his head. I needed to see the person I had fallen for and not this emotion-less mannequin.

"Wait up," I heard him call out, stopping me in my tracks. Despite everything, his voice still made my heart beat faster.

"How are you, Malik?"

"I'm fine. Hurry, you don't want to be late for class."

I didn't know how to reply and I desperately tried to bridge the gap between us.

"Let's bunk class and just walk today. We could listen to music or grab something to eat off campus."

"You know Hari sir gets really mad when his students miss his classes."

I couldn't stop myself from blushing at how he remembered my schedule even though I knew he was blowing me off.

"Fine," I murmured reluctantly, resolving to give this another shot in the evening.

I had cleared up my schedule and was ready to finally get him to open up to me tonight. I had made up my mind that if it didn't happen today, it wasn't going to happen at all, and that would be the end of it. As much as it broke my heart, I knew that it was required, and I had no other option left. I felt a sinking feeling in the pit of my stomach and I tried to imagine life without him. He had become an accustomed element of my day and it felt like it would be near impossible to forget him. I had left him the sordid 'We need to talk' message and I nervously waited for him in his room.

He entered his room after his class ended, as punctual as ever. At least some things never changed. His forehead glistened with sweat as he came in hurriedly.

"What's wrong, Raina?"

"Aryan, how do you feel about your mother?"

"What do you mean?"

"Are you okay?"

"You know I am," he said looking visibly less anxious.

"That's just it. I don't! I don't know anything about you anymore. How are you feeling, Aryan? I have no idea and I'm getting sick of it."

"Raina, I've told you multiple times that I'm fine. I don't understand what else I can tell you to make you feel better. I'm dealing with this in my own way."

"Talk to me about how you've been feeling. You just lost the most important person in your life. You can't just be fine, that's not the way it works."

"You don't get to decide what works for me, I don't need this. Let's talk about something else."

It was now or never. I had to say what I was most scared of, even though it meant that things would change between us forever. He was finally looking at me, but he was still so distant. I couldn't be in a relationship that was driving me crazy. I gathered some courage and looked into his eyes, wishing that my Aru would come back. I intertwined my fingers with his and glanced at him again, pleadingly. He looked at me with the same stoic expression on his face and I felt physical pain in my chest.

"Aru, if you can't tell me how you feel, then I'm not doing a good enough job being your girlfriend. It means that you don't trust me with your deepest thoughts. I know you lost your mother, but that doesn't mean you lose yourself. You're not the same person you were a year ago and I can't do this anymore."

I could feel the tears well up in my eyes and I didn't want him to see just how much this was tearing me apart. I grabbed my bag and ran out of his room as fast as I could without walking into any of his furniture. I wanted to see how he was reacting, but I was too scared to look at him, just in case he made me change my mind. Even worse, I was afraid to see the same indifferent expression on his face. It was raining outside and I felt like I was playing out a scene from a movie. The rain poured down whilst the night sky seemed to engulf me. I knew that the icy water should have been pricking my skin, but I was numb from the events of the night. I had relied on him too heavily and now it felt like my universe was ending. It was gravity that had started this in the first place. I had been existing in my cosmos until he pulled me towards him like we were made of the same matter. Who was he to not change when even the stars didn't stay the same. And as numerous as the stars, I could feel my heart breaking into a hundred billion fragments.

"Raina, wait. Please."

I almost fell in relief as I heard his voice calling out to me. My knees buckled as I turned around and I started sobbing heavily, not being able to stop myself anymore.

"I need you. Please don't go. Come to me, my baby," he said holding his arms out wide.

That was all the signal I needed and I ran into his arms, breathing in his scent. It somehow made me cry harder and when I looked up at him, I saw that he was weeping as well.

"I love you," he whispered into my ear, tucking my wet hair behind it.

I froze where I was standing. This had been the first time he had said those words to me. We hadn't even brought up the concept of love before, but we knew how much those words meant to the both of us.

He started kissing my ear and I fell into him completely, weak with all that had happened.

"I love you too, Aryan. I really do."

He looked into my eyes, this time with love. I could see it in the way he looked at me. Aryan Malik loved me. And I loved him too. I felt like I could give up my whole life for him without blinking an eye.

He pressed his lips against mine passionately and I thought about how this was the first time we had kissed in the last three months. I put my arms around his neck and he scooped me up, taking me to his room. I felt secure as he carried me and I realized that he was the one I wanted to lose my virginity to.

"Let's do it, Aryan," I whispered into his ear.

He met my eyes with an innocent surprise that just made me fall in love with him deeper.

"Are you sure, my love?"

I brushed my lips against his in reply.

"Oh, Raina!"

He continued kissing me and undressed me deftly. I couldn't help but wonder how many times he had done this before. The thought dissolved as he touched my left collarbone gingerly. I looked up at him reassuringly, making sure he knew that this was okay. Hell, this was more than okay. Nobody had ever made me feel this way. I knew that we were still kids at the mere age of twenty-two, but every bone in my body ached with the love I felt for him.

10

Naked and exhausted, we blissfully lay in each other's arms. As I was about to fall asleep, I heard Aryan mumble something under his breath.

"Have my adequate skills in bed left you speechless, Aru?" I teased.

"More than adequate, I would say. But listen to me, I haven't been fair to you. I haven't talked to you about my feelings and you didn't deserve that."

"Talk now?"

"Yes. I've been living with the belief that if I talked about it, it would be real. As long as I kept it within me, I thought that I would just wake up one day and it would all be a dream, you know?"

"Yeah, I do. I know you must be going through the most difficult thing in the world, but that's not the way life works. Wishing something hard enough won't make it come true and it's definitely not healthy. You have to accept it at some point and start grieving, Aru. I'll be there for you, every step of the way."

"How Raina? How do I accept that my father has to sleep alone in the same place where he shared his life with that beautiful woman? How do I accept the fact that my very own mother passed away?" he said choking.

"I'm so sorry, Aru. I wish I could take the pain away from you. You still have a family. You have me. As long as I have a say in that, nobody's going to take me away from you."

He nuzzled his face into my hair and took a deep breath. I could tell that he was holding back from crying.

"Cry Aru. Let yourself cry."

"I can't."

"Why? Do you think it'll make you less of a man? Fuck these gender roles and do what you fucking want to."

He looked at me taken aback for the second time tonight.

"Raina, I don't believe in any gender roles, but I just never have and I don't know how to."

"You never have because you were told not to. It's me. Look at me. You can cry. Let yourself go."

With that, Aryan started breaking out into small sobs. Soon he was howling while I held him. He cried until he fell asleep and I waited until I was sure that he was okay.

The next morning came scented with roses. That is if anyone's ever figured out what roses actually smell like. I tried sniffing them as a kid just as I had seen girls in movies do, but I was thoroughly disappointed in the ordinary scent that wafted my nose. Roses may not have a particular smell, but they were there on the desk with a sticky note attached.

I couldn't find tulips. I love you.

I held them up and sniffed them anyway. Still no scent, but that didn't matter. If Aryan had made the effort to wake up early and find roses for me, I would love these roses, scent or no scent.

I walked back to my dorm holding the roses in a dream-like state. Before I could enter my so called room, I heard Anya and Savi's voices from the floor above. My friends could never keep it quiet and that was probably the reason why the entire second floor was always complaining about them. I entered the room and smiled at them happily.

"What's wrong with you?" Savi laughed at me.

"I just had a good night, that's all."

"Oh my god, you totally lost your virginity!" Anya exclaimed rushing over to hug me.

I blushed but continued to remain quiet. Aryan and I hadn't discussed whether it would be okay for us to tell our friends and so I wasn't sure if I should confirm the happenings of the night.

"I'm so happy for you Raina! Honestly, I thought you guys would be breaking up soon. He seemed like he was lost in his own world. Is that phase over now? I hope you used condoms. What did it feel like? It was your first time, no?"

They were my best friends in IBII. I had to tell them. I'm sure Aryan wouldn't mind, but I wasn't sure what I felt about him telling his guy friends. Living in India, I was very well aware of the double standards that came with having sex. Guys were players, but girls were sluts. It was strange how society encouraged guys to have sex whilst they also heavily discouraged sexual women and homosexuality. Who were the guys supposed to be sleeping with?

"Raina, tell us the details now!" Anya whined.

"Yes, sorry. It was amazing. I hope that phase is over, Savi, and of course we used condoms. I told him I was ready to do it because I realized that I'm in love with him. He told me that he loves me too. He finally opened up to me about his mother last night. I really do love him, guys."

"This requires major celebration. Raina, my girl. We're drinking tonight," Savi said.

The girls enveloped me in their joyous bubble and I welcomed the feeling of being in love.

11

June: Second Year of IBII

I couldn't believe that my journey in IBII was almost over. Hand in hand with the nostalgia came the pressure of the finals week. All the students scampered around with books in hands, waiting to get another coffee so that they could continue studying all night. I've always been a planner and I planned the shit out of the week. Assigning an hour to each chapter, I sat in Aryan's room making sticky notes so that we wouldn't forget our individual commitments. What came as a surprise was how easily he distracted me even when he was trying not to. I hadn't been able to account for this in my planning and if I wasn't careful, I would be lagging behind my packed schedule. I glanced up at him and tried to ignore how much I liked the way he furrowed his brow while going through some page that was particularly tough.

"I know I'm attractive, but jeez, stop," he said catching me looking.

I ignored him and continued studying. He had already been scolded by me for not letting me adhere to my plans. I was determined to ace my exams and if I could just concentrate slightly more, I was sure I would. It was already three in the night and I had just one more chapter to cover before I could revise. Yes, I was one of those people who needed to revise. Aryan, on the other hand, wasn't too keen on being assigned revision hours. He had complained about how I was taking the exams too seriously, masking the anxiety he felt. It was weird how every set of exams felt more significant than the previous set.

When I was in the eleventh grade, my parents had told me that it was now or never. I had to study and this would be the last time I ever had to worry about spending all my hours buried in books. Then when I went to college, I heard the same lecture all over again. Now, two years later, I was feeling the same emotions and telling myself that this would definitely be the last time. I stopped to ponder at that thought for a while. After this, the real world would run its wheels and it was my job to not get trampled under them. I may never have to appear for an exam again, but I would also have to say goodbye to lazy summer holidays and hello to responsibilities. Albeit the stress, earning for myself would be a whole new experience and I was exhilarated. I couldn't wait to be unaccountable to my parents. I would no longer have to explain the bills of my spoilt fits of shopping which I only needed after sad days. I could also begin to return everything that they had given me. Coming from a privileged and caring family, my parents had always given me all that they could. It was time that I started fulfilling all of their wishes and desires. I also wanted to spoil

Radhika and live up to the image of the successful elder sister. That is if she ever spoke to me again. Her silence had been deafening and there hadn't been much I had done about it. I liked to believe that she would realize soon enough that I wasn't the one to be blamed for her rejection. She had always been an irrational child and sometimes needed to stroll down the wrong path before she reached the right one. She needed to see that I loved and supported her, but she also needed to do it on her own. If I pushed her further I would just end up pushing her away. She liked handling things the way they came to her, while I liked controlling my future myself. I had already decided what I would do with my first few salaries. The first would go to the needy, the second to my parents and the third to Radhika. The rest would always be divided in half. The first half for my needs and the second half for my savings. What did I say about planning? I needed it to make sure that I was in the slightest bit of control over the unpredictable future. I resisted the urge to ask Aryan what he would do with his own salary, even though I was pretty sure that most of it would go towards his restaurant. He looked focused on his current text and I didn't want to sidetrack him. Besides, I had my own chapter to finish.

What's weird about finals week is that in the moment, every minute feels like an hour, but once it is over, it feels like the whole week passed by in a blur. I read this theory once that as we grow older, time flies by faster for our minds. It makes sense because with every passing year, the portion of the life that we have already lived grows larger. While comparing our current year to the portion of life we have lived, the current year keeps growing smaller in comparison. As you turn five, you just have four years to look back on, so one year doesn't seem too short when compared to four years of memories; but as you turn forty, one year compared to thirty-nine years of life feels awfully short. It's a mathematical theory so I don't know if it makes sense to everyone, but it really explained why every year seemed shorter than the past year to me.

I walked out of the class where my last exam had taken place and sighed in relief before I was bombarded with my friends asking whether my answers matched theirs. Right on cue, Anya and Savi hurried over asking me about my sets and discussing their doubts animatedly. My paper had gone well and I didn't have many questions that needed clarifying. They grabbed my question paper and started noting the questions I had circled and marked.

"Even I hated this question!"

"Yeah, this one stopped me for a while, but on the whole, it was pretty easy, no?" Savi looked at me.

"Yeah, my paper went well. You guys?"

"Yeah, it wasn't too bad. I'm not failing for sure," Anya giggled.

Savi and I shook our heads at her and couldn't help but join her contagious laugh. We probably looked like silly school girls, but we didn't care. We felt unstoppable and free.

"Where's your Aru?" Anya asked me teasingly.

Oh shit. I had completely forgotten. Where was he? I scanned the crowd, but couldn't see him around.

"I hope his exam went well. Let's find him?" I asked the girls.

They nodded and we walked around, trying to spot him amongst the mass of excited students. Aryan was sitting under a tree looking over his paper. I sneaked up behind him and closed his eyes.

"Guess who?"

"Give me a second, babe."

I sat next to him while he scoured over his paper. While patience isn't my greatest trait, I waited quietly until he was done.

"Was the paper not good?"

"It was better than average. But no, I wouldn't call it good."

I knew that when he said better than average, he meant that he wasn't getting full marks, but that he would also be amongst the top ten. His intelligence was one of the many qualities that had made him so endearing to me.

"I'm sure it wasn't as bad as you think, Aru."

"You're right, I'm probably over-thinking. How does it feel to be free, Miss Raina Kapoor?"

"As long as I'm free with you." I blushed at his usage of my full name.

"Well, that's ironical. Freedom and relationships don't usually go hand in hand."

"Oh, shut up, Malik."

He shut me up with a kiss.

12

Our graduation party was held the night following our final exam. It was supposed to start at 10 p.m. in IBII's main hall and was rumoured to go on till 2 a.m., which was a big deal for the conservative city. Anya, Savi and I had already stocked up on booze and we were stoked to let loose before the placements started. It was our last night to reminisce and celebrate with our entire batch before we got busy in our individual lives. Not that I cared for many people in this batch besides Savi, Aru and Anya. These three people had become my own in the short span of two years. While I had felt isolated by the distance, they had been my pillars of support. My only other interactions had been forced with Savi's friends and about a hundred of Aru's. I knew their names and faces, but they were barely people I would miss once I graduated. Nevertheless, it was a good opportunity to bid them farewell tonight. The convocation ceremony was going to be filled with hustling and crying parents, so really, this was the only opportunity.

I called Savi and Anya to my room at night to decide which dress to wear for the night. The last time I went to Delhi, I had brought along a few of my favourite outfits that I usually saved up for the biggest parties, but since this was a special occasion, I was more than willing to sacrifice one of the dresses. I started out with a black bodycon dress that had a mesh back. The girls hooted with approval as I gave them a spin showing off the back. The next dress I tried was more on the sober side, white with a sweetheart neckline. The third dress was bold with two cut outs flashing my waist. The fourth, the most daring of them all entailed of red material that clung to my skin accompanied with a plunging neckline. I tried it on nervously wondering whether it was too much.

"You have to wear this; you'll be the hottest girl there tonight!" Anya gushed.

I glanced at Savi as she was the more practical one.

"Yes, I absolutely insist Raina," Savi nodded in approval.

"Also, don't get ready in Aryan's room tonight. Let him see you for the first time on the dance floor. I want to see his reaction."

"Why? That's absurd. He can see it in the room."

"No, she's right. He'll see the whole process of you getting ready. It won't be as special then."

"Well, I haven't gotten ready with you guys in a while," I pondered.

"It's done then. We have to pregame here anyway," Savi smiled.

I sent Aryan a text informing him that I wouldn't be coming to the room so he could start drinking with his friends. Savi borrowed my white dress which complimented her tan skin beautifully and we assigned a short, tight and black playsuit to Anya. Satisfied with our choices, we proceeded to discuss our heels. I had brought my only pair of standard black pumps so I didn't have much of an option. I thanked my stars that black went with every other colour. Anya revealed the existence of her immaculate shoe collection to us. I knew that I probably wouldn't be able to squeeze my feet into her tiny shoes, but that didn't stop me from trying. Savi agreed to do my make-up and contoured the Kardashian out of it. Putting on the final touch of my red lipstick, I was good to go.

"Let's start drinking," I cheered.

We had bought two bottles of tequila and one bottle of vodka. It was more than enough to last the entire night. I usually tried to avoid mixing, but I was ready to go all out tonight. We started with diluting our drinks with Coke, but soon we were drinking straight out of the bottle. With four drinks and four shots, I knew I was drunk.

"Listen!" Savi shouted drawing our attention.

"I love you guys!" she slurred.

"You know, a lot of people in my school were mean and put each other down. But you guys? Never. You always want the best for me," I slurred back.

"You guys, I'm going to cry. We can never lose this," Anya joined us.

My planner instincts kicked in as I looked at the clock in my room. It was 11:30 already and we were getting late.

"Let's go and show this college a good time,"

The IBII hall had been decorated with black and white ribbons across the room and matching helium balloons floated near the ceiling. The room was packed with inebriated students swaying their bodies. IBII had done its students proud.

We walked to the middle of the dance floor, moving our bodies to the beat. Surrounded by the mass of people, it felt easy to get lost in the crowd. We were joined by a few friends and in moments of intoxication, they felt like a part of my inner circle as well. I greeted them with excitement as we grooved collectively. After a while, Anya joined a separate group of friends on the other side of the room. Savi and I continued to dance until she was approached by a semi-attractive guy. They went to dance intimately in a corner of the room where a lot of other couples had collected. The other half of my couple was unfortunately missing. I tried calling him, but failed to find network. I decided to leave the hall and walk until I reached a place with connection. I rushed outside the room, stumbling in my heels. My calls were still not going through to him. I wondered if he had even made it out of his room yet. Aru wasn't a heavy drinker, but he had told me that he had bought some amazing bottle of whiskey for the night. I hoped that he hadn't gotten himself into any trouble. Finding myself losing balance, I stumbled to a place where I could sit and continued calling him. I have realized that when you're under the influence, you often forget the appropriate number of calls and texts that should be sent. A tall and large guy soon joined me in my spot.

"Hey Raina," he smiled.

"Hi Varun," his face rang a bell. He was in my quant class, but we had never actually had a conversation.

"You know we've never spoken, but man, we should have."

"What?"

"I always noticed you though," he said leaning in.

Feeling uncomfortable, I attempted to get up, but was stopped as he placed a firm arm on my wrist.

"Where are you going?"

"To find Aryan."

"You're still dating?"

"Yes," I answered coldly.

"I'm sure he won't mind, just sit with me for a little while longer," he said almost pushing me back.

"I have to go," I said urgently. His behaviour had disabled my disorientation and I felt as sober as ever.

He got up, his tall figure leering over me.

"I'll go with you."

He matched my pace, making small talk on the way. I continued responding in monosyllables. He suddenly grabbed my waist and pulled me towards him.

"What the fuck are you doing?"

"Come here, babe," he said pulling me even closer. I winced at the sound of my favourite nickname coming from the wrong mouth.

"Let me go!"

"I know you want this," he grinned one inch away from my face.

I knew he was going to try kissing me, and I felt sick to my stomach.

"No!"

He ignored what I said and came closer anyway. Pinning my arms to my side, he had left me with no way of escape. I contemplated kneeing his balls, but I couldn't find the space to do so. Kissing my cheek, his breath was right above my lips.

"*Stop!*" I shouted.

He grabbed my ass and almost put his lips on mine. I screamed and I saw his body flying to the ground. Aryan was here! And he was punching Varun's limp body.

"It's okay Aru, I'm safe."

Aryan continued punching Varun until his hand bled.

"I'm safe. It's fine," I said pulling him away.

"No, it's not fine. What he did was not fine. He didn't even ask for your permission. He cannot take advantage of you, or of anyone, for that matter."

"Yes, but it's over now. Let's go," I pleaded realising that he would get himself hurt.

"Raina, I'm so sorry I wasn't here."

"It's not your fault."

"It's not yours either, okay? People like him deserve to go to jail."

"How far would you have taken this, Aryan? If I hadn't stopped you. You know Varun is bigger than you. He was drunk tonight, but normally he would have hit back."

"I would be willing to go to any length to protect you."

"Aryan!"

"No, I'm serious. I would fight until every bone in my body was broken to protect you."

I glanced at him sideways, realising the gravity of what he had said. Aryan would give up his own life to keep me safe.

13

The seriousness that lulled over the college was a stark contrast to the colourful posters that were stuck on the walls. The big companies had arrived with promises of salaries, houses and cars. The banners contained slogans such as 'Work at iJob, we place you first', 'BHC protects you' and 'Indi, the best bank in India'. These banners were of course irrelevant as we had already done our research and knew what we wanted. Unlike Indi, some of these firms were actually the best in India, and most of them provided great opportunities for both management and marketing, the specialities of IBII. Finance also promised a lucrative career, but after much thought, I had decided to go into management. I was aiming to work at one of the banks, so that I could climb up the ladder to becoming the manager of a branch. I had already made my dream list and it consisted of four organisations: GlobalCity, HFC, Platinum and Soltra. Aryan had made a similar list, but I knew he wanted to work in the food service. His plan was similar to mine. He also wanted to go into management, so that he could control a chain of luxury restaurants someday. Losing his mother had created a burning passion for this dream and I was sure that he would stop at nothing to achieve it. It made sense for us to be in managerial roles because we were both good with people and had a knack of controlling chaotic situations. Our hard work had paid off in our results, placing both of us in the top ten percent of the college. Our futures depended on our upcoming interviews with the companies of our dreams. Aryan and I pretended to interview each other, so that we could prep for the tough questions that might be thrown our way. This also brought up where we would like to be placed. I knew that Delhi would definitely be my first option. Delhi was followed by Mumbai because of the family I had there and subsequent to Mumbai was Bangalore, a city I loved visiting. They were all metropolitans and that would be sure to raise some eyebrows. If given no other option, Aryan was conflicted about whether he'd rather work at a restaurant outside Delhi or a firm in Delhi. I had a feeling he would choose the restaurant.

"What if I choose Goa? The tourism builds the profits of the restaurants there. Would you come with me?" he asked jokingly, but I could tell that it was a genuine concern.

"I don't know, Aru. We don't have to decide right now," I said brushing off the topic. I truly didn't know what I would choose. I could just hope that we both got the companies we desired in the same city. I wasn't sure how we would do at long distance, but I would be up for giving it a try. I knew that the odds weren't great, but I believed that the connection we both had was uncommon, to say the least. We could beat the odds, if need be.

The day of the placements, I wore a blue saree with dangly earrings. I looked like a professional and presentable adult after I managed to pin my hair down. The humid weather and rain made my hair messy and I had to use intense conditioning to settle it. I tried to ignore the building anxiety and walked to the hall where my future employers sat waiting. I hoped to god that it wouldn't start raining before I got there.

My first interview was with HFC and it was probably the best out of all my other interviews for the day. Indi came a close second as the man had told me that he would love to have me work for the company on the spot. The workers from Platinum had been intimidating as they stared down at me while asking questions related to career, academics and life. I had stumbled when they asked me about my priorities. Although it took me a minute, I replied saying that learning, building and revolutionising the company would be my top-most priority. This was almost entirely true. While I was saying the words, I had realized that my first priority would be Aryan and then the company. Being an ambitious woman, I was shocked at how smitten I was. I hoped that he would be willing to go to the same lengths for me. Surprisingly, none of the companies had questioned me about the cities I wanted to be placed in. On the whole, I was satisfied with the process and awaited the results eagerly. They had informed us that they would tell us in a week.

"How was it, my love?" Aryan asked me grinning.

His interviews must have gone splendidly as well.

"Good, I think I may get one of my top choices," I said grinning back.

"You're smart, Raina. I'm sure you will."

"And you?"

"Most of them were good. Some were okay. One guy asked me technical questions about food. I did not know that one of the most famous pizza toppings in Brazil is peas," he laughed.

I held his hand, reaching out to kiss his cheek.

"I decided something today."

"Hmm?"

"I want to be with you."

"It's been two years and you just decided that?" he pouted.

"Shush. You know what I mean. It's okay if you don't get Delhi. Hell, it's okay if you get a job anywhere in the world. If it makes you happy, I'd come with you. As long as we fly back home every weekend, of course."

He rolled his eyes and pulled me towards him.

"You can drive me crazy, but you do know that I'm deeply in love with you?"

"It's been two years and you just decided that?" I winked.

14

December: One Year after IBII

It was one year after the graduation ceremony and we had comfortably settled into the blanket of security that Delhi provided us. It was our home and it was the place that both of us had known for the first twenty-one years of our lives. After college, Aryan had received a placement offer from a famous luxury restaurant, Dolce, in Delhi. He would be the manager of its outlet in Hauz Khas. I had received offers from multiple companies, but my main choices had been Platinum and HFC. They both had branches in Delhi and were willing to give me a sufficient salary. Platinum was a smaller company as compared to HFC. This had brought to me its own set of advantages and drawbacks. Platinum wasn't as well known as HFC, but it would also be more flexible to the changes I wanted to implement. I had decided on Platinum and was now a proud employee with a salary of two lakhs per month. It was a decent start and was more than what I had been expecting. Although I still lived with my parents, I had decided to stop asking them for money altogether. I could buy whatever I needed and would still have money left over to spend on them. Aryan was still slightly dependent on his father as he was saving most of his own salary for his future business plans. Our offices required us to reach work by 10 a.m. and we were only let off by 6 p.m. Sundays were working for him, but I had the whole weekend to myself. We had created our own routine and we adhered to it religiously. I thanked god for his blessings each day. I wasn't always such a grateful person, but one day, Aryan took me to a slum that was close to his building. He greeted the kids with familiarity and they asked him to a game of football. Aryan and I were on opposing teams and his team won the game and my heart. Watching him play with the kids created an unexpected blend of love and arousal within me. There's just something about guys playing with kids. It's universally acclaimed to make hearts melt. After the match, we sat with the children as Aryan distributed the chocolates he had got from home. We asked the children what brought them joy and they gave us simplistic answers such as food, housing and even colour pencils. The experience taught me the value of how much I had, not only in terms of finance, but in terms of family and relationships. Speaking of which, things were great between me and Aryan. My parents and Aryan's father had gotten along during the graduation ceremony and all of us often met up for dinner. At the ceremony, I had been worried about the impression Aryan would make, but he had conversed with them about their hobbies, likes and dislikes splendidly. My mother had taken an immediate liking to him and even my dad hadn't been immune to his charms. I'm sure if Radhika had come, she would have loved Aryan as well. We still weren't on speaking terms and it almost felt like she wasn't a part of the family anymore. The new family I had found had filled in the gaping hole she had left and I had begun to love every second of it. It also made going out with him so much easier, because my parents almost never said no when I asked for permission. I knew that I was old enough to technically not need their permission, but for them, I would always be their little girl. That and the fact that I was still living under their roof gave them the right to still say no to me when they felt like it was unsafe or unsuitable. I tried to listen and not rebel as long as they were fair about their decisions. Radhika used to take my side when it came to going out, but I always knew that it was so that she would also get permission for the same outings when she was my age. I had learnt that she was happy at Carla and I wondered if she thought of me at all.

The girls and I had realized that the ceremony would be the last time we would be together in Indore. Savi had chosen to work in Delhi for a while, but Anya was taking up an offer in Kolkata. She said she couldn't refuse the perks, but she made us promise to keep in touch. It was difficult at times, but so far we had managed to stay updated on the big things. Savi had become a permanent part of my group that was integrated with my friends from home as well as Aryan's. Charvi and Mahima were also active members of the group. Mahima and her boyfriend had broken up halfway into my second year in IBII. I had been crushed because I had been hoping that my relationship would last as long as hers did. I had also been crushed just because my best friend was in pain. The whole week had been a mess of tears and Skype movie sessions. I had eaten chocolates in my dorm room while she ate ice cream from the room of her house. Charvi had practically lived there for the week. They eventually got back, but broke up two months later. I had seen it coming, but had tried to be as supportive as I could. According to me, once a couple breaks up, the sanctity of their relationship reduces. The unit that seemed so invincible suddenly becomes as fragile as everything you encounter in life. If you break up again, the sanctity reduces once more. You also realize that there's a power struggle between you and your loved one. One takes up the role of a reacher, while the other takes up the role of a settler. A reacher is someone who had to reach to find the other because they probably couldn't have found someone like them on any other given day. The settler is the one who could have gotten anyone but settled to be with their current partner. You can guess which one is more invested. Once those roles are found, they become more and more evident in your relationship, until the settler finally becomes sick of the reacher. I had been in a relationship like that and had made a strict rule for myself to consider the relationship over at the very first break up. I wanted to be with someone who couldn't bear the thought of being without me, let alone ending it when convenient. I was willing to not give up until I was given no other choice, and I expected the same in return. I had tried to convey the same to Mahima after they broke up for the second time, and she had dejectedly agreed. Although she wasn't ready to date yet, she had moved on now and was just another healthy and happy person.

If you've lived here all your life, you'll find that anyone you meet here has probably been close to one of your old friends at some point in time. Upon coming back, we had found that Dhruv from my circle was dating Zara from Aryan's. That had resulted in a couple of double dates and had made the interaction amongst our friends that much easier. We had a tight group of reliable and trustworthy people here, that we met for various events every other weekend. I'm aware that Delhi is a large city, but I'd like to believe that all our hearts are connected. After a few encounters on the bustling roads, I had learnt that the people may seem brash on the outside, but they're sure to melt if you treat them with respect and kindness. Possibly because they're just not used to it. However it may be, I belonged to the city and it belonged to me as well.

It was Saturday which was always 'Aryan day' for me. It was the only day he got off from work. I had a neat rubric for the days of my week assigned to the people who were important to me. I was usually burdened by work through the weekdays, so I spent my Fridays with my friends, my Saturdays with Aru and my Sundays with my family. Savi made fun of me sometimes for having my life too well planned, but ironically, this controlling instinct was something that I couldn't control. Any second I found myself free, my brain would start worrying and planning the rest of my time to optimise its usage. I thoroughly believed that life was too short and I had to make the most of every second that I was given. Albeit my attempts to schedule the day, Aryan had told me that he had a surprise for me and that it was a big one. I'm sure that it had something to do with the fact that it would be our three year anniversary at midnight. I had bought him a watch that he could wear to work every day. It would also serve as a great reminder of me. The date we had started dating was engraved on the back in Roman numerals. I had considered getting words engraved as well, but I liked the minimalistic and elegant look the Roman numerals gave. I had also made him a small card which had become our very own tradition. It started with our first year anniversary when he ordered ingredients online and snuck into the university kitchen to cook for me. Never having dated someone for this long, I hadn't wanted to make too much of a big deal out of it. I had seen men struggling to remember dates in my favourite movies and I had assumed that Aryan would be the same. On the day, he ended up preparing everything, while I came empty handed. Embarrassed, I had made him a small card while he cooked the meal. He had said he loved it, makeshift and all.

"What's the surprise, Mr Malik?"

"You know your perfume drives me insane, Ms Kapoor."

"Well you're driving me insane with the suspense," I said satisfied that my perfume had the effect I had predicted.

"Do you have a card for me?" he smiled.

"Not until you reveal your surprise."

"Have it your way, but I have a feeling that my surprise might just be the slightest bit better than yours today."

What did he have planned?

"Let's eat then."

He took me to a restaurant that was close to my office, although I had never heard of it before. It was a quaint but romantic place, lit up solely by candlelight, and beautiful fairy lights draped across the walls. I noticed that it only had tables with the setting for two and that each table was visibly further from the others. This was the perfect place to come for our date as it gave us all the intimacy that we required. While the waiter took our order, we coyly played footsie under the table. A wave of pleasure ran through me as I realized that footsie still gave me the same thrill I had felt when we had just started dating.

"The candlelight highlights your beauty. It illuminates your face and did you know that you shine brighter than the moon?"

I was taken aback by his intensity and didn't quite know how to react.

"So pretty, yeah?" I said sticking my tongue out at him.

"Even like that," he laughed.

I usually convinced him to split the bill, but today, he wasn't taking no for an answer. Eagerly waiting for the surprise, I decided not to fight it too much.

"I have to take you somewhere."

"For the surprise? Can't you tell me right now? I want to give you your gift," I whined.

"No. Patience baby. You can give me yours now," he said knowing that I wouldn't.

We walked down the road of restaurants and cafes to where he had parked his car.

"It won't take long," he promised.

I sat on the passenger seat while he drove me to the mystery. I loved riding shotgun because ever since I had been a little girl, I had seen my mum sit next to my dad while he drove. They would quarrel jokingly while Radhika and I cheered them on from the back. Sitting next to Aryan made me feel the same way.

"We've reached. Come," he said getting out of the car and rushing to open my door. We had reached a resident lane and I wondered if he was making me meet someone. He took my hand and I noticed that his palms were sweaty.

"Close your eyes."

I did as told, too intrigued to challenge his dominance. We had parked near a house and he was guiding me inside. I opened my eyes to a hallway lit with tiny candles. The ambience was similar to that of the restaurant. Red tulips were placed in a vertical line leading up to a room. At first glance, most people would have thought that they were roses, but I knew he had placed the flowers that were special to us. Tulips were the first flowers he had given me in IBII. Each tulip was accompanied with a polaroid of our time together. I would say that Aryan and I were a romantic couple, but this was extreme and my mouth dropped open at the thoughtfulness of it.

"Follow the tulips."

The sweetheart had even put our pictures in chronological order from IBII to Delhi. I followed the path quietly, wondering what else was to come. Had he rented this house for us the spend the night at? The tulips led to a desk with a note on it. I lifted the note and read it aloud: *Look behind you*. I turned around and the sight left me stunned in silence. Aryan was sitting on his knee, holding up the most beautiful ring I had ever seen.

"Raina Kapoor, I have loved you every day that I have known you. You're a woman who inspires me, protects me and loves me for who I am, and I want to spend the rest of my life thanking you for it. There's nobody else that I can ever be with again. I want to build my future around you. I want to raise children with you. I'm not always sure about everything, but I am so damn sure about you. Would you make me the happiest man in this universe and marry me?"

"Yes," I yelled, not having to stop and think about it for a second. I loved him. Oh, I loved him so much.

We later lay in bed after celebratory sex. He told me about how his dad had bought him this house long back, but had never revealed it until recently. Aryan planned to pay him back for it once he was settled, but he wanted us to live here until then. He had even asked my parents for my hand and they had agreed. We had never discussed marriage in depth and I sure as hell hadn't been expecting this from the night.

"I told you my surprise would be better," he grinned.

15

January: Three Years after IBII

"Are you seriously carrying me over the threshold?" I laughed as Aryan swooped me in his arms. We were entering our house for the very first time. The location was perfect because it was close to both our offices. Aryan worked in Hauz Khas while I worked in Gurgaon. This was somewhere in the middle, Vasant Kunj. His dad had wanted to gift it to us, but Aryan had been firm about paying him back. His dad had then decided to give us the second best gift he could think of. He hired an interior designer to fill the empty space. It had been an excellent decision on his part as we both didn't have the time required to design a home. We had not been allowed to visit and were only consulted for minor decisions such as the types of mirrors that we needed and the rooms that required television sets. Many couples don't believe in having a television in their room, but for us, it was a straight yes. I could imagine spending many of my nights curled up against Aryan, while we watched all sorts of movies. He hated to admit it when we were with his friends, but he liked romantic comedies as much as I did, and maybe even more. I couldn't count the number of times I had caught him watching *Titanic* on television, claiming that it was the only movie he could find. Not that I blamed him, it was heart-breaking and my go to period movie. That and *The Notebook*, of course. I had forced Aru to stay in many nights with me while we sniffed and fought over the last piece of pizza during my period. He was always a gentleman, pampering me with chocolate and massages.

I still couldn't believe that I was married to him. It had all gone by so fast. The day after he had proposed, we had met our parents for dinner. They had been overjoyed and excited the entire dinner, planning the venues, dates and people. We had been engaged for an entire year in order to decide on the best of everything, and more importantly, to give ourselves time to prepare for married life. The actual wedding had taken place without a hitch on the same date as our four year anniversary. Although we had a huge reception, Aryan and I decided to have only our closest friends and family for the actual wedding. I had grown up watching movies where girls walked down the aisle and I wanted to incorporate that into our wedding. We decided that I would walk down the aisle to the mandap where the phera ceremony was to take place. We planned to recite our own vows before we circumambulated the fire. We also made sure that it happened during the evening, when everyone was awake and lively. Thankfully our parents hadn't protested too much, they were just happy watching us be happy. I had joined dance classes as well as pilates to shed off extra weight. Shopping had been a nightmare, but I had finally decided on the most beautiful and elegant bridal wear that I could imagine. My hours of hard work had paid off with the love and admiration that I saw in his eyes when he looked at me. He had been dressed in a sharp suit and had also joined a gym to get fitter. We both wanted to look our best for the most special day of our lives. Our wedding ceremony had taken place in a private resort in Goa, near the beach. Our wedding planner had decorated the whole resort and beach area with white tulips. Everything had gone exactly the way I had imagined it to be. Before I had walked down the aisle, Savi had gotten me a bottle of vodka to swig shots from. I hadn't felt any second thoughts about him or the wedding throughout, but I needed the liquor to relieve the tension so that I could enjoy my evening instead of worrying about what could go wrong. I could safely say that surrounded by everyone I loved, I had celebrated the happiest day of my life successfully. At the end of the exhilarating and tiring day, we went to bed together in a private villa inside the resort. Our honeymoon had to wait until after our wedding reception, which was to take place in Delhi. We had let our parents plan the reception and they had gone all out. Using it as a bonding experience, they had planned it together meticulously. The event had everything from ice sculptures to fondue fountains. They had decided to call all their friends and acquaintances to announce that their dear kids had gotten married. When I confronted my mum about going overboard, she had defended herself by saying that she had waited for this day all her life and deserved her moment. She hadn't interfered in any of the decisions for the wedding ceremony, and so I had let it slide. The reception included more than a thousand people, and the both of us were expected to greet each and every one. We spent the entire night hugging our parents' guests and accepting their well wishes. We also sent our friends to the bar frequently to get drinks for us. By the end of the night, we were drunk and rushing to the airport to finally start our honeymoon in the island of Bora Bora.

It had been surreal, staying in our private cottage surrounded by the bluest ocean that I had ever seen. Our cottage had a sign in front that said, 'Welcome Mrs and Mr Malik'. Every glance at it caused butterflies in my stomach. I couldn't believe that I would be called Raina Malik now. A tingle ran down my back every time the staff referred to me by my new name. The cottage also had glass floors with the view of swaying coral and swimming fish.

We ordered heaps of food to energise ourselves after making love to each other. Delighted by an array of prawn, lobster, ice cream and fudge, we had savoured every exquisite bite. We had also gone exploring and trekking to various waterfalls. After lunch, we sat outside our cottage in the middle of the freaking blue ocean. The hotel had installed a beautiful balcony area complete with swings, hammocks and chairs. We used the space to relax and to occasionally throw each other into the water. Well, it was mostly Aru who had done the throwing, but I had succeeded in pushing him while he slept on the hammock. During the evenings, we often got massages with the view of the glistening water. The whole thing had felt like a dream to me and I would have been willing to stay there for another month, but with work piling up, we both had to get back to real life eventually. So here we were, with Aryan picking me up before we entered the place where we would spend the rest of our lives.

16

I drew in a sharp breath as I glanced over the house. I couldn't
believe this was the same place where Aryan had asked me to
marry him. The interior designer had outdone herself with the
elegant furniture and ornaments she had chosen. Our parents
must have given her a good description of who we were as people
because she had found the perfect balance between luxury and
comfort. I looked at Aryan's stunned expression as he took in our
home.

"Wow."

"Wow."

"Did you gain weight in Bora Bora, my love?" He teased and
I realized that he was still carrying me.

"Put me down then."

"Not until we reach our bedroom."

She had chosen a plush white bed for us with ebony wood
drawers on both sides. A white fur carpet was placed in front of
the bed and I was almost scared to set foot on it, worried that

the soles of my shoes would taint the snow white. All our floors were wooden, giving our house a homely feel to it. My favourite part of the room had to be the glass wall. There was one wall that had entirely been dedicated to the view outside. It flooded the room with sunshine and showed us the garden and the buildings outside our house. It may not have been the view of an ocean or a valley, but I liked it all the same. Aryan placed me on the bed and bent down to kiss my lips.

"Welcome home, sweetheart."

I snuggled into his arms.

I later discovered that all our bathrooms had black marble walls and cream coloured granite sinks. She had even taken the time to put a wooden wall in one of the hallways with pictures of the both of us and our families. I noticed that the wall contained pictures from each of our family vacations, our graduation ceremony, our events at IBII, our personal gatherings from home and of course the pictures from our wedding. Everyone important had been placed on the wall. She had really made an effort to set up the whole house and I was sure to recommend her to all my friends if they ever needed a decorator. I walked on to explore what she had done with our balconies. The balconies also had wooden flooring and were lined with glass. The edges were decorated with deceivingly real looking plants. I realized that they were fake because we probably wouldn't have the time to take care of them while we were at work. Our kitchen was already equipped with dishes and cutlery. I was so glad that I hadn't had to design the house by myself. Just the amount of planning that was required to turn a house into a home would have driven me crazy, I'm sure. I had seen my mum do the same for our house when I was a kid. I had marvelled at the time and effort required for what seemed like a fun activity. She had gone from shop to shop to find the best deals for even the smallest items. I swear I could have visited fifty furniture shops just to find the right curtains for my room and I hadn't even accompanied her on most of her trips. The designer had left me with nothing to do. This house was great exactly as it came. All that was left to do was move in my own things from my old house.

You've been MIA! Call me.

My phone buzzed with another message from Anya. In all the excitement, I hadn't found the time to check my phone since the wedding. I had only spoken to my family to assure them that I was doing fine. Every single one of my closest friends had made it to the wedding, but they were all eager to know how married life was treating me. I had been the first one in the group to get married, and from what I'd heard, the most predicted one as well. I anxiously unlocked the cell anticipating the number of texts I must have received. A few names popped out amongst others. Anya, Savi, Charvi and Mahima had all called and texted multiple times. I made a plan to meet Savi, Charvi and Mahima for dinner before they had my head. Anya had flown back to Kolkata after the reception, so I had to wait a while before I could see her again. After finalising my plan with the girls, I sent quick voice notes to Anya trying to describe the bliss I felt. With the dinner and work the day after, I would have no time to move my things in yet. I had to stop by home and pack a suitcase that I could use for the week before I made it to the restaurant. Aryan was jet lagged and was fast asleep. I was just going to send him a text about my whereabouts when I realized that I could literally write down a message on paper and leave it on his bed. Although we had already almost lived together in IBII, I had gotten used to living in different houses once we got back. Taking advantage of the married life, I sprayed the note with my perfume and left for my old house.

"You're late," Savi frowned at me as I entered the Asian place she had chosen.

"And you've tanned!" Charvi greeted me.

"You look lovely. Your skin is glowing," Mahima said hugging me. I grinned at them, delighted to share the details of my trip. My skin had to be tan and glowing from the glorious massages, facials and hours under the sun. Bora Bora had been twenty-eight degrees even in the middle of January.

"Is it the sex?" Charvi giggled.

"Is married sex any different?" Mahima asked.

"Why are you late?" Savi asked bringing up the topic of my punctuality once more. Aryan and Savi were both sticklers for punctuality and often gave me shit for being even a couple of minutes late.

"It was impossible to get my mother off me. She was as excited as you are and didn't let me leave until I answered all her questions."

"Did you meet Radhika?"

"No, she flew back to the States after the wedding."

"What was up with her? She barely looked at you."

"I know. She's still holding that grudge."

"It was your wedding. Isn't it time she got over that?"

I shrugged trying to hide how hurt I had been by Radhika's indifference towards my marriage.

"Maybe we should talk to her. She is our best friend, after all," Mahima laughed.

When we were all kids, Radhika insisted that she was as close to Charvi and Mahima as I was. She didn't have any close friends of her own, so she hung onto mine. I was too young to understand and got highly annoyed when she wanted to tag along for our plans. I asked her to confront the both of them and ask if they were her best friends. She complied. Refusing to upset my little sister, they went along with the whole thing. Fed up, I finally typed out fake messages on the notepad on my laptop. Fabricating the conversation of them complaining about Radhika, I showed it to her, hoping that she would get the hint. Not convinced, she continued trying to go out with them until she grew up and made friends of her own. Charvi and Mahima joked about it with her, whenever they came over. That was all before the great fallout, of course.

"Tell us about the honeymoon. Don't leave anything out," Charvi winked at me and I smiled at her for changing the topic at hand.

It took me an hour to give them the itinerary of all my days until they were satisfied. We then moved on to discuss what they had been doing in the time I had been gone.

Savi was still dating Aditya, whom she had met in a club, four months after moving to Delhi. She filled us in about how she had met his parents for the first time, but hadn't made a great impression. I reassured her that they would love her once they got to know her. I knew that Savi's sarcastic demeanour was just a front hiding her sensitive side. She wasn't the most social person and I could imagine parents not taking an immediate liking to her. Her charm would eventually work its way to their hearts, just as it had with Aditya. I was glad that things were getting serious because I had helped her kickstart their relationship. She had brushed him off when they had first met, thinking that he would just be interested in casual sex. He had found her number from a friend of mine and had messaged her in the morning saying that it was lovely meeting her. Savi had been taken aback and had called me nervously asking what it meant. I had told her to go with the flow and get to know him while she was at it. She had continued calling me with information about his latest messages, which soon turned into intel about their latest dates. Aditya seemed like a nice person and I had been rooting for them throughout.

Charvi told us about her latest problems at home. She didn't get along with her mother and they often fought about the amount of time she spent with her stepmother. Her father had gotten married to the woman awfully soon after his divorce with her mother and it must have been tough on the mother. She felt replaced by her in the lives of both her husband and her daughter. This caused her to lash out at Charvi, but she still didn't take out the time to spend a day with her. Charvi was stuck in the middle and didn't know which one to confide in. The mother who had raised her but had never made an effort, or the new family member who was always wonderful and warm towards her. Charvi was getting teary talking about their latest fight and so Mahima steered the topic towards work. She was trying to make it as a professional photographer and was currently working for a fashion magazine. She met divas sometimes and told us about their antics and demands. The stories were bizarre and cracked us up.

By the time we were done with our meal and conversation, the jet lag had started kicking in. All I wanted to do was to go home and sleep next to my husband.

17

December: Four Years after IBII

I was on my fifth call to Aryan and he still wasn't picking up. He had been especially busy the last two months and had only spent a few minutes with me each day. He had gone to office from Monday to Sunday, returning home as late as 2 a.m. I had been frustrated by the end of it and demanded that he take some time out for me. I hated being that person, but I had a secret to tell him and hadn't been able to find the right time because of his schedule. He had promised me that that night he would leave early so that we could grab dinner and catch up. I had been excited to finally spend time with him and had dolled up for the occasion. I was dressed in a simple but sexy black dress that showed off my cleavage. My breasts had noticeably increased in size and looked especially good in the dress tonight. I felt like a young girl trying to impress a crush from school. You shouldn't have to feel like this, I scolded myself. You're married, for god's sake. I couldn't exactly blame Aryan. He had wanted this restaurant all his life and he was good at what he did. He had been under a lot of pressure lately, because he was thinking of buying the whole chain of restaurants. Although he started with managing just one branch, he had been so efficient that they had promoted him to managing a couple of branches in the same area. He had appointed someone else to his previous branch and had successfully taken over the higher position. After two years, he was promoted in management again, but this time he was in charge of the whole chain in Delhi. Dolce only had restaurants in our city, and to control the entire enterprise was a big deal. He had worked really hard to get where he was now, but he believed that it was time to get his dream. He knew Dolce inside out and wanted to own it. He had been planning on giving the owner a deal. He would either buy off the chain for a sufficient amount of money or he would leave his job. It was a big risk, but he was willing to take it.

"I make all the important decisions for Dolce, Raina. The business will fail without me and Suraj knows that. I am going to give him more than the company is worth and then the restaurant will finally be mine completely. It's a deal he cannot refuse."

This is what he had been planning for his whole life and I had been as supportive as I could, but tonight, I needed him to be here for me. I had been waiting at our table for an hour and he was nowhere to be found. The families that had come in after me were starting to leave and I was losing my patience. When should I leave? I decided to give him another half an hour. If he wasn't here until then, I would go back home.

Doubts started to flood my mind incessantly. What would happen if Aryan bought Dolce? Would he have to spend more time at work or less? I know that he was working especially hard right now to make the offer more appealing to Suraj. He promised that it would all be over soon, but wouldn't owning an enterprise be more work than trying to own one? Hundreds of livelihoods would become his responsibility. If someone were to sue the restaurant, they would be suing us. And what would happen if he lost his job? Finding a job in our economy wasn't as easy as advertised. It took time and effort. Would his ego be able to take a hit like that? And what about money? I was earning well for myself, but I wouldn't be able to support our household on my own. As the clock kept ticking, I analysed more situations in my head. If both our careers were on the line, who would leave their job? I don't think I could ask Aryan to do so. I don't know whether he would if I did. I couldn't leave either. I loved my job and I hadn't studied all my life to become a housewife. What would we do? Worrying thoughts continued bothering me as I waited.

"I'm so sorry." I could tell from his face that he looked excited, but that angered me further.

"Where were you?"

"I'm here now, baby. Let's eat."

I looked at the menu in front of me, even though I had already read it ten times. He couldn't just walk in and act like everything was okay.

"This is unacceptable. I needed you. I've needed you both these months and you haven't been there for me. Is this how things are going to be? Are you going to keep chasing an impossible dream?" I don't know why I said it, but I couldn't stop myself. I knew it would hurt him and I glanced at him, waiting to see how he would react.

"I got it. I got my dream and I was so eager to tell you."

"Good for you," I said, sarcasm dripping from my tone.

"Why are you ruining this for me?"

"Just go!" I snapped.

"What?"

"Don't come back to the house. I'm sure you would be happier with your job!" I shouted, unable to stop myself again. My insecurities had created a dark cloud over my head and I found myself pushing him away.

"Raina? Are you serious?"

He was whispering, which was a stark contrast from the decibel I had chosen to use.

"Yes."

"What did I do? I'm sorry," he said looking at me earnestly.

"You're an asshole," I said and walked out.

I didn't allow myself to cry until I was out of his sight. I couldn't believe this was happening. We had never spoken to each other this way, let alone spend a night apart. I had never insulted him before. Please follow me. Please. I continued walking, hoping to hear his voice behind me. I was greeted by silence and it was all my fault. He had just wanted two months to himself. I could give him that for being the loving and loyal husband that he was. I didn't know what had taken over me at the dinner. I continued crying until I reached home. I checked our bedroom, wishing that he had somehow reached before me. He wasn't there. Where could he be? I took my phone out and sent him a text.

Come home please.

He was there in the next fifteen minutes. I rushed into his arms, sobbing like a child.

"I'm sorry I was so awful to you."

"I understand Raina. It's okay," he said making me cry harder.

"No, you didn't deserve it."

"What were you so worried about, my love?"

He was being so nice to me when I had just been the worst.

"I was just scared that you wouldn't have time for me anymore. I was really excited about tonight and when you didn't show up, I started telling myself that this would be a daily thing. Worries and fears clouded my head to the point that I couldn't think straight. This is not who I am."

He was still holding me, but hadn't responded.

"Please don't give up on me," I whispered.

"Hey. Are you listening to yourself? I would never give up on you, Raina. You're my fucking wife. That's what's special about love. When you love someone, you don't give up. The both of us? We're one unit. We're in this together."

"The three of us. I'm pregnant."

18

September: Five Years after IBII

Saying that the months that had led up to the birth of our baby girl had been tough, would have been an understatement. Now, as I looked into her hazel brown eyes and played with her tiny nose, I knew that every second of pain and fear had been worth it. Aryan and I smiled at each other knowingly. We had created this pure and angelic being together. We were going to take one step at a time and give our girl the life she deserved. When I had told Aryan that we were going to have a baby, we had both cried and embraced each other the entire night. We weren't sure how we would make the time to raise her with our busy schedules. We weren't sure whether she would sleep in our room or have a room to herself. We weren't sure whether she would be our first and last. We weren't sure about the religious values we wanted to teach her. We weren't sure about a lot of things, but we were so god damn sure about her. Without a doubt in our heads, we had known that we wanted her. Of course, in the beginning, we didn't know whether we would be having a girl or a boy. It goes without saying that we would love our child, no matter their sex, sexuality, likes and dislikes. A parent loves his or her child unconditionally and I don't think another love like that exists. What Aru and I have is so special, but as hard as it is to admit, it comes with strings. My heart would always care for him, but if he ever cheated on me, I know that I wouldn't be able to go back to him. My child, on the other hand, could do whatever he or she wanted and would always have me. He or she could hurt me or hate me, but I would sacrifice every cell in my body for his or her happiness.

"Do you think it's a girl or a boy?" Aryan had asked kissing my stomach.

"I have a feeling it's going to be a boy."

"Really? I think it's going to be the most beautiful girl and she's going to have all your features."

He may have been right about the first part but he was definitely wrong about the latter. I looked at my baby's face noticing every feature. We had the same pointed nose and brown eyes, but her lips were her father's. Her black hair also resembled Aryan's. I wanted her to have his kindness and his wit as well. He was looking at her with such genuine adoration. I knew he was going to spoil her like he spoilt me. Even though it's illegal to determine the baby's sex in advance, I really wanted to do the whole cake shindig, where you cut a cake open and the colour of your slice reveals the sex of your child. We couldn't have that and so Aryan had promised me that we would throw a huge celebration party once our baby was born. We didn't believe in the gender norms of pink for girls and blue for boys, but I knew that my mother had picked out scores of pink balloons and ribbons for the event. This party was supposed to be especially exciting because we would officially be announcing her name to our loved ones. Not even our parents knew what we had decided yet. Knowing that we wouldn't have much time to ourselves, they had happily welcomed the opportunity to throw another party for us. We had given them the freedom to decide the menu, the music and the decorations, but we had been strict about the venue and the guest list. They knew that we wanted it to be held in the comforts of our own home with only our immediate friends and family. Ironically, we ended up spending most of the night in our own bedroom, too attached to our baby girl to even leave her out of our sights for a second. After we had announced her name, we had let everyone gush over her for a while. Soon after, I made the excuse of feeding and took her back to the safety of our room. Even though I trusted everyone at the party, my protective motherly instincts kicked in and I wanted to keep her away from the noise and the chaos. The world could chatter and dance all it wanted, but I was happy to be holding my daughter's hand in the privacy of my own room. Aryan's usual social nature had also taken a turn and he had been even more eager than me to spend time with her alone.

"I'm never going to let you go, baby," he babbled to her.

"It's going to be impossible for this one to keep a boyfriend, huh?" I laughed.

"When the time comes, we'll buy a gun," Aryan joked back.

I thanked god for my beautiful family once again. All throughout my months of pregnancy, Aru had been my rock. Whenever I had doubts or freaked out about minor issues, he had been there to calm me down. In the beginning, when I had started to gain weight, I had asked him if that made me less attractive to him. He had given me the correct answer pacifying all my insecurities.

"Sweetheart, watching you create life and give birth to our baby has made me fall more in love with you than I even knew was humanly possible. Nothing could make you less attractive to me."

He had known when to take the reins and when to let me be in control. We had made most of the decisions together, but when we were in disagreement, he had trusted my insights like they were his own.

Before she was born, our main name options had been Riya and Meher. Riya Malik and Meher Malik both had a ring to it that we liked. I had expected to place one of the names to her when I finally got to hold her. But at the hospital, none of the names had felt right for her. I had been overwhelmed with how pure and innocent she was and I had wanted a name that reflected that.

"I know that we were deciding between Riya and Meher, but what do you think about Tahira? It means clean, pure and holy and that's what our baby is. Doesn't she look like a Tahira?"

"Tahira Malik?"

"If you like it," I had said, although I was already attached to the name.

"It sounds a little bit like a mixture of Tara and Heera. She's become the star of our lives and she's surely as precious as a diamond."

I had been overjoyed that he was considering it.

"Tahira Malik," he had said again, giving me the indication that he accepted it.

"Tahira Malik." I had repeated in agreement.

19

May: Ten Years after IBII

"What do you want to do, sweetheart?" I asked my five-year-old daughter on our trip to Bali.

"Cycle?" she giggled, sending a warm rush of happiness to my heart.

Raising Tahira with the love of my life had been the greatest joy that god could have given me. We were here to celebrate seven years of marriage and take a break from our hectic lives back at home. Tahira was growing up to be a gentle, kind and smart girl and her parents couldn't be more proud. She had befuddled us with her mature and calm behaviour during times of conflict. There weren't many conflicts that a toddler could be involved in, but once, a boy from school wouldn't stop pulling her hair. Instead of hitting him back, her response had been to patiently explain to him why he mustn't hurt other people. When he had refused to comply, she had shared her tiffin with him and asked him to be friends. It turned out that he was only being nasty because he didn't have that many friends to begin with. He had agreed and now came over for play dates every month. Tahira had shown us her consideration even when it came to animals. Her school was walking distance from our home and she had a habit of bringing in injured birds and puppies on our way back. She would nurse the creatures and cry until we agreed to take them to a vet.

One day after I had come home from work, she had asked me why I came to school less than the other parents. I had tried explaining to her how I had to go to office and not all parents chose to do that. She had understandably been confused about the concept, still asking me to volunteer for her carnival. I had known that volunteering required a couple of hours a day, specially right before the big event. That was also the time when work was as busy as ever, with everyone hoping to impress the boss in time for their Diwali bonus. It wouldn't have been practical for me to commit to something that I knew I couldn't give my hundred percent to. Tahira had continued insisting that I sign up, refusing to listen to reason.

"Hira, why is this so important to you?" I had asked her.

"I just miss you when I'm in school, Mommy," she had replied, causing tears to well up in my eyes.

I had subsequently driven to her school the very next day, surprising her once her day got over. I had spoken to her teachers and received excellent feedback about the patient and well-mannered girl that she was. My next week had mainly consisted of running out of my office during lunch hour to spend time at the school, where I could help organize the event. I barely got to eat and although I wouldn't like to repeat that particular week, I was rewarded with my daughter's smile every day.

Sometimes when I was feeling low, she would say the most heartfelt things, giving me hope in the good of humanity again. I knew that every parent must feel this way about their children, but I really believed that she would do amazing things for the greater good of the world when she grew up. It had become an idle pastime for me and Aryan to sit and discuss what we thought she could become. We were ambitious parents and we ranged from astronaut to writer.

If Aru and I ever argued in front of her, she would stare us down with her big eyes and make us apologise to one another. Even though it was our seventh year of marriage, the spark between us was still aflame. Married couples are often worried about the seven-year itch, but that didn't seem to be an issue for us. We couldn't get bored of one another because we always desired to spend just another minute with the other. Work and Tahira had us completely exhausted and we only got real quality time during the weekends. This trip had been necessary for us to rejuvenate ourselves before we were back to our schedules in Delhi. Here, we had the luxury to wake up in the afternoon and go for a swim in the ocean, working up a big appetite for lunch. Aryan was teaching Tahira how to swim and even though she wasn't the athletic type, she was catching on slowly. After half an hour of lessons, she would dawdle back to the shore and continue making her sandcastles. We had bought her dolls and action figures and she combined them both, cooking up stories of their activities in her castle.

"Hira, try one more time?" Aryan had pleaded with her.

"Papa, no," she had said, wagging a finger at him, fully aware it would make him laugh.

She was dressed in a yellow sundress and I swear that her smile shone brighter than the sun. I had thought that I wouldn't be one of those parents whose lives revolved around their children, but Aryan and I were obsessed with our little girl and couldn't get enough. During my maternity leave, it had taken Savi weeks to drag me out of our house and go for dinner with her and the girls. Even though Aryan was at home, I had fretted the whole time with most of my attention on my phone, waiting for updates from him. She had eventually convinced us to let her babysit while we went out for a movie or a meal.

"You need this, and besides, it'll be great practice for me and Aditya. Think of it as a favour for me, but please go," she had urged. I was used to working now, but I had cried on my first day back to office, unable to imagine not being around her for as long as eight hours. Aryan had stayed home to take care of her that day and had built a day care system in his workplace soon after. We both understood the value of giving time to our daughter and made sure that she never felt alone.

"Mama?" she asked, pulling on my top. Oh yes, the cycles.

"Yes Hira, let Papa finish his shower and then we'll go," I beamed at her.

"Did I hear you call Papa?" Aryan said, picking Tahira up.

"We want to go cycling, Aru."

"Then cycling we shall go," he said placing a kiss on each of our cheeks.

Pedalling through the streets of Bali, I could taste the traces of salt in my hair which was constantly brushing against my face.

We had no route or itinerary to follow and we cycled without any constraints. The wind was blowing on our skin and the weather was deliciously pleasant. Somewhat like the weather you get in Delhi around September when the summer heat has faded but the cold hasn't set in yet. Tahira cycled alongside us, proud that she could keep up. I can imagine how picture perfect our family of three would have looked like to the people on the paths. As long as I had these two in my life, I had nothing else to ask for. They were my strength and my weakness. We continued cycling way past Tahira's bedtime and she was exhausted, succumbing to sleep as soon as we reached the villa. Aryan tucked her into bed while I dressed for dinner.

"We did good, my love," Aryan said clinking his wine glass with mine.

"Exactly what I was thinking," I said, blowing him a kiss.

20

March: Eleven Years after IBII

Nobody ever wakes up thinking that their world is going to explode that day. It's probably the most illogical belief humans hold. We see bad things happen to people every day, but we assume that these are just stories we read in newspapers. We never think it could happen to us. We never even imagine the possibility, fearing all that we have to lose.

The fifteenth of March. The day everything changed.

I woke up a few hours after the sun. Yawning lazily, I was delighted that I had got to sleep in. I would be taking a personal day and I planned to spend the next few hours deeply relaxed in a spa. I hadn't really wanted it in the beginning, but Aryan had given me an all-expenses paid spa day for my birthday and I had never got the time to use it. It had been a year and the gift card would expire in a month.

"You need it and this is the perfect excuse," he had argued with me while gifting it.

He repeated the same words again last week.

"Don't waste the money, love. Your face looks so tired, it hurts my eyes to watch you," he had joked, convincing me to give in.

I had looked over my schedule meticulously and finally found a date when the office wouldn't miss my presence. He was right, I was in dire need of a facial and my aching back longed for a deep tissue massage. I decided to listen to my body, my heart and my husband and take a day off. I had made an appointment for 10 a.m., disappointed that they didn't open before that. I wanted to be done by four so that I could go grocery shopping and then cook for my family. I wasn't that great a chef and that left Aryan to do all the heavy lifting. Our help usually didn't stay till dinner and that left us with takeout from his restaurant on most days. He insisted on cooking during the weekends and this would be a pleasant surprise for him. I didn't know too many recipes, but I could make a mean taco. All I had to do before my appointment was drop Tahira off to school. Aryan walked her every day as it coincided with the time he headed to work, but today, I had asked him to let me do it. I would even buy her some unhealthy breakfast from the bakery that we crossed on the way. Her face always lit up while licking the chocolate off her doughnut and she looked adorable with smears of it on her nose. Checking the time, I realized that it was eight already. I had to start getting ready so that she wouldn't get late the first time I dropped her. Just five more minutes, I thought, tucking myself under the covers once again. My alarm blared and I got up grudgingly, finding my slippers. This seemed like a sundress day and I started scrounging my wardrobe for a comfortable but pretty dress. I found a white tube sundress that I hadn't worn in a while. Slipping it on, I put on some lipstick and hurried to get my daughter.

"Where's Papa?" She asked me sleepily. Like mother like daughter.

"I'll be taking you today, Hira."

"Mama!" she cheered and I couldn't help but hug her.

"I love you so much."

She flashed a toothy smile at me and I held her hand, guiding her to the door.

We were almost skipping our way to the bakery. It was so convenient that we had found a good school just five minutes away from home. Aryan and Tahira both got to sleep more and we never had to worry about how we would take her.

"What's happening in school, baby?"

"Mama, so Alia and I are best friends now, and we share our tiffins every day. We like going to the red swings because everybody doesn't go there, but sometimes Ali is there and he doesn't get off and so we have to wait really long," she babbled.

I asked her questions about Alia and Ali, enjoying her aimless chatter. We had reached the crossing before the bakery and I could see that Tahira was getting even more excited. I held her hand, but before we could cross, I realized that my sundress had gotten stuck to a nail on an electricity pole next to us.

"Hira, one minute. Wait here while I get this off."

She was still talking and I looked away to free my dress. I was pulling it from the nail when I heard the brakes of a car slam near me. Next, I heard screaming. I looked up and realized that Tahira wasn't next to me anymore. No. No. No. Where was my baby?

People were crowding near us, but all I could see was her backpack next to the car. No. This couldn't be happening. No.

Tahira! I tried to scream, but no sound escaped my throat. My legs were frozen where I stood and I couldn't move my body. I could only look at her backpack and hear my heart beat as if it would jump right out of my chest. I urged my legs to run to her rescue. My body got over the shock as my maternal instincts kicked in. I sprinted to my daughter's body, picking up her limp body in my arms. I realized that a warm liquid was dripping on my arms. The warm liquid was red.

"I've called the ambulance, didi," someone said near me.

"Call the police!" Someone was shouting further away.

"I'm so sorry. She came running from nowhere," I heard a voice pleading close to my ear.

I could sense a crowd near us, but I couldn't focus on anything. It all seemed like a blur of faces and noises around me. People were yelling things and crying, but none of it registered. All I could do was look at my daughter's face and pray to every force in the universe that she would be okay.

21

"Is she going to be fine?" I asked the nurse for the tenth time in a row.

Words that didn't make much sense to me had been thrown around as soon as they had taken Tahira away from me. All that they had done was scare me senseless. I had been able to register only a few words and they didn't make me feel any better. Traumatic head injury. Contusion to the head. Bruised brain tissue. Torn blood vessels. Surgery. Hearing these terrifying terms wasn't doing me any good, and so I had decided to only focus on finding out how soon she would be out of surgery. Every passing second felt like a decade and I thought my head would explode sitting in the same place. I started pacing back and forth to give myself something to do. I continued praying silently in my head, begging some supreme power to make this go away. I tried making deals with the power in my head.

"I'll give up drinking, working, hell even living if you make sure she's fine," I whispered to myself.

I would be willing to give up anything in the world to ensure my daughter's well being. Where was Aryan? How would he react? I needed him to reach the hospital so that I could fall into his arms and cry my heart out.

"Is the surgery over?" I asked another nurse crossing me.

"We'll inform you when it is, please wait," she said talking to me patiently, with pity in her eyes.

I took support of a wall as my knees started to feel weak again. I probably looked like I was about to pass out myself, with my torn and bloody dress and sunken eyes. I glanced at the door that had a flashing red light with the threatening letters 'ICU' under them. I had tried peeking through the door, but had just been ushered away. My little baby was in a room getting operated on by strangers. She would be so scared when she woke up. I had to make sure they let me in as soon as the surgery was over. I had to go protect my daughter and let her know that she wasn't alone. Never in my life had I felt this helpless. If only there was something I could do to make it better for her. My breathing was getting ragged and I had to keep reminding myself to stay strong for Tahira. She wouldn't want to see her mother like this, I scolded myself. I took a deep and troubled breath as I counted another second passing by.

"What happened?" I became alert as I heard Aryan's voice from across the hallway. I rushed to him, finally letting myself sob. My sobbing soon turned to wailing and I couldn't let any words out. I kept stuttering and heaving and he started patting my back to calm me down.

"Talk sweetheart, talk. Where's Tahira? Is she in school?"

My blood froze as I realized that the doctors hadn't informed him about her surgery.

"They told me that there's been an accident. What happened, Raina? Are you okay?" he said holding me close.

"Aru. Aru." The words were too horrible to say.

"I'm here Raina. Tell me."

"Tahira."

He immediately became motionless at the sound of her name.

"Tahira? What's wrong?"

"She's in surgery," I said as the tears started streaming again.

"What happened? Is she okay?"

"Car accident. I don't know, Aru. The doctors haven't told me anything useful. I don't know what to do."

I looked at him hoping for comforting words, but he had started running. He stopped a nurse standing outside the ICU and desperately began asking questions. I heard her repeat the same words she had said to me.

"Trauma to the head."

"Contusion."

"Bleeding"

"Swelling."

"Operation."

"We don't know. We will inform you."

Did she not realize how empty that sounded?

Aryan was frozen outside the door, his face agape with shock.

"But how?" he was stammering. It broke my heart watching him gasping for air, similar to how I had been reacting just moments ago.

"Raina, tell me what fucking happened?" he said taking me aback with the sternness in his tone.

I recounted the events of the day, willing myself to not break down again.

"The one day you took her to school," he snapped at me. The tears started rushing in and I looked for anything else to blame. I couldn't be responsible for this. I was a good mother and good mothers didn't let this happen to their daughters.

"I looked away for one second. I told her to stay. I don't know how this happened. She just ran in front of the car."

"This is why I always hold her hand near a road. She's a child, what the hell did you expect?" he said raising his voice.

We all have different ways of reacting to grief. If this was his, so be it.

"I'm sorry. She'll be fine. I know she will," I said grasping at his hand. He pushed mine away and went to sit near the godforsaken door.

Our parents had also been informed and soon they were rushing down the hallway. My mother entered with bloodshot eyes, wearing an oversized t-shirt. She had clearly been in bed when she had been called. My father was wearing his office attire and was holding her protectively. I could tell that he was stopping himself from crying so that he could be strong in front of her. As soon as they entered, my father gave her a look of understanding and she stopped sobbing immediately. He had probably instructed her to hold back her emotions in front of me. Watching the whole scene just made me cry harder. They rushed towards us, asking details of the accident and feeding us with words of consolation that they seemed to believe in wholeheartedly. They told me that she would be out and healthy soon, even though they had no way of knowing. Only the doctors knew and they still weren't telling us anything. Aryan's father came in half an hour later with the same teary eyes. He reacted like Aryan, running around and finding staff to interrogate. He returned after receiving the same information and started researching the surgery on his phone. After fifteen minutes of scrounging, his face fell and I couldn't bring myself to ask. He put his phone away and told us that it would okay, even though he looked like he didn't believe it himself.

We continued waiting outside the neurosurgical ward, but still heard no update. My father had worry lines etched on his forehead and he decided to take up the job of feeding us. He went to the hospital cafeteria, bringing back juice and sandwiches. I couldn't swallow the tiny bite I took, knowing that Tahira hadn't eaten yet. Every time we asked, they told us that she was still in surgery. What were they doing to my daughter that was taking them so long? My poor Hira.

"You're going to make yourself sick," my mother pleaded.

"You have to eat, Raina," Aryan's father chimed in.

Aryan had still not uttered a word to me and was chewing on his sandwich quietly. I forced my throat to swallow, resisting the urge to hurl. My body needed to know about her before it could take care of its own functions. Giving up on forcing me to eat, my mother had retired to a corner, praying again. I decided to join her and repeated what she told me to.

"Have faith, beta," she kissed my forehead.

The doctor operating on Tahira walked out of the ICU in the same second. Had the praying worked? Please let the praying have worked. Mum had asked me to keep faith and that's what I needed to do. I looked at the doctor's stance and he seemed to be walking dejectedly. No. He was just exhausted after operating for so long.

"Can we see her now?" Aryan pounced at him.

"I'm sorry."

"Is she still in surgery?"

"We did everything we could."

"She's going to be fine. Tell us she's going to be fine," I begged the doctor.

"We couldn't stop the bleeding. She crashed during the surgery. We tried to resurrect her, but it didn't work."

The reality of what he was saying hit me and I felt my legs unable to take my weight anymore. Our parents rushed to help me up, and they placed me on a bench. Aryan was still standing at the same spot, not breaking eye contact with the doctor.

"This cannot be happening. She's only six years old. Take care of her. Please. She's the only child I have."

"Her heart stopped beating, Mr Malik. She passed."

22

I never expected two simple words to bring me such intense grief. Although his voice had been strained, he had said the words and left to attempt to save another patient. A patient who actually had a chance. Tahira never got that chance. She had fought till the end, but eventually, her body had given up. Those words haunted me every second, replaying through my head like a song on repeat. Except I couldn't stop them. I couldn't press pause and push them out of my head. The words just kept on running, manifesting a home in my mind. It's funny how those words had a completely different meaning until her death. I couldn't believe that I was thinking of the death of my very own daughter. Kids always rejoiced when someone passed. For them, it meant that they had given an exam successfully. It brought even more happiness to students giving entrance exams. How could such joyful words be used in such a dire situation? I couldn't accept that my daughter was dead. I wouldn't be able to accept it. She was so young and had such a happy life in front of her. She had only done so much and she had so many experiences left that she hadn't got the opportunity to be a part of. All our well laid plans for her crumbled with those two words. She didn't get to graduate from school. She didn't get to experience college life. She didn't get to find her passion. She would never fall in love and get married. She would never birth children. She hadn't even travelled yet. She hadn't seen most of the world. She would never eat bread in France and pizza in Italy. She would never get to meet her idols. She would never even enjoy a night spent with her best friends. I felt so sorry that I couldn't give that to her. If only I could have seen her and stopped her from running. If only I had never worn that stupid sundress. I shouldn't have told her about the bakery. She was a child who was bound to be excited at the prospect of chocolate. I should have known that she wouldn't wait. I should have never taken a fucking off from work. Forget work, I was unable to even stand up and walk to the kitchen. It was my job to protect her. I was her mother and that was my only job and I had failed miserably.

I deserved this for always running off to my office when I could have spent another hour with her at home. I deserved this for not being careful with her that day. This wouldn't have happened if Aryan had walked her. He always knew how to take care of her. He didn't deserve this. Hell, I don't think anyone in the world deserves to go through this pain. Except me, who couldn't even take care of her own child. My sweet and innocent daughter was dead. What did she do to deserve this? It's so strange how I spent so much time planning out my days, but I was unable to plan for the most devastating day of my life. Tahira and Aryan owned my whole heart, and without her, it felt like someone had taken out a chunk of me. I felt hollow and empty and I had no idea how to deal with something like this. She had been my only child and the apple of my eye. Our friends had heard that Tahira was in the hospital and had already gathered at the house. We had just entered, but I was already missing the echoes of her laughter. God, I couldn't enter her room and look at all the dolls she had carefully placed in her doll house. I couldn't eat, drink or even breathe properly. I could see the haze of faces around me, but I couldn't fully comprehend what they were saying to me. I could hear people wailing, but I couldn't even bring myself to cry. They had stopped by to give us their condolences and they were doing everything from saying words about Hira that made people cry even harder, to bringing us food to eat later. My parents had taken charge of the house and were addressing the well wishers and their concerns. My mother had whispered something about moving in to take care of me, but it just made me feel even more suffocated. This wasn't normal. I needed to grieve alone and these people weren't letting me do so. I just needed to run away to some place that didn't hold Tahira's childhood. Some place that Tahira hadn't just been in. I could almost see her holding my hand and looking at me with her big brown eyes. She would probably ask me why all these people were crying and would want to help them out. I couldn't let her see me cry. My tears would just upset her. I had to go some place where she couldn't see me.

"I'm so sorry. I'm so sorry, Raina. I don't know how this could happen," I recognised Savi's voice near me.

"Take me away from here," I urged her.

She gave me a look and quickly packed a few things. Dodging all the guests, we rushed out of the house before anybody could stop us. Once we were out, I started running. I couldn't stop myself even though I wasn't running to any place in particular. If I stopped, it would be real. My daughter's death would become real. So I kept running. Savi tried to follow me, but I had long gone past her. I ran and ran to get away from the heartbreaking situation at home. I didn't know where to go, but I just knew that I had to run. I could feel the sweat dripping from my forehead and blending into my tears, but I couldn't care less. I would continue to run until I was far away from all those people in my home.

More than an hour had passed and I could feel my pace slowing. I knew I would need to stop soon and I realized that I had reached a locality I recognised. Although I hadn't noticed my surroundings while sprinting, I had involuntarily run to my old house. I could see it now, just a few steps away from me. The house I had lived in before IBII and before Aryan. The house I had grown up in. This house hadn't known any pain. This house knew me and was what I needed right now. I hoped that my parents still hid the key behind the box with the bell. I reached for it and my fingers felt the coldness of the metal. It was still in the same place. I unlocked the door and went to my room immediately. Tired from the running, I collapsed into my bed. I was grateful that my parents had left my room exactly the way it used to be. Most people would have renovated and created a study or a bar, but they had left it with all its belongings intact. I held my childhood teddy bear called Honey and finally let myself cry. Once the tears came, they wouldn't stop. My body convulsed in the pain of losing my daughter and I wailed and howled until I couldn't breathe anymore. I shouted for god to bring her back and threw plates at the wall when I wasn't given a response. The house was empty and I was glad I could break down without people watching me. After I was done being angry, I slowly cleaned all the pieces of glass and climbed back into bed again. I shut my eyes and continued crying softly until my body gave out, lulling me into slumber.

I was woken up a few hours later by the sounds of my noisy family. In despair, I had forgotten about how worried they would have been about my absence. Aryan was already going through so much, I didn't have to put him through trying to find me as well. Apparently, Savi had called all my close friends and asked them to help scout for me in my favourite locations. They had gone to all the places I went to frequently, including my office, but they had been unable to locate me. Finally, Savi had guiltily gone to my mother, telling her that she had lost me. She had given her the run through of the places they had checked and my mother had asked if they had gone to the Malviya Nagar house. Savi sheepishly admitted that that hadn't been a place that had occurred to her. Mum had driven here immediately to find me sleeping in my room. She had informed the others that I was safe and had sat with me while I slept. That's the thing about mothers. They always know what's best for their children. Even though I didn't. Soon, all our loved ones had changed their grieving place from Tahira's childhood home to my childhood home. I could hear them scuttling about the house, trying to make our lives easier. If I weren't so racked with sorrow, I would have appreciated the effort they were putting in. I looked for

Aryan, but I couldn't see him around. Was he still at our home in Vasant Kunj?

"Where's Aryan?" I asked my mother.

"He needed some time alone, just like you did," she said looking away.

The words made sense, but the expression on her face didn't. She was avoiding making eye contact and looked guilty. Maybe she felt bad for not bringing him for the support she thought I needed.

"It's fine, Mum."

"Are you fine?" she asked me, knowing that I wasn't. How could one be after the death of her daughter? I doubt I would ever be fine again. Maybe one day this would become an experience that I tucked at the back of my head, but every memory that I would make after this, couldn't possibly compare to the days I had lived up to this. The days when I had been ignorantly blissful believing that I was invincible. The days when my daughter had still been alive. How could I make a better memory than the memory of her small face gazing up at me with admiration? Every time I closed my eyes, I could imagine her big eyes and her wide smile. I could see her cheeks getting pink while she ran around the house. I could smell her hair after it was freshly shampooed. I started getting overwhelmed again and knew that I had to get away. This time, I would just rationally tell everyone that I needed to sleep in my own bed without them looming around me. More importantly, I needed to be with Aryan.

After a few attempts of convincing everyone that I didn't need them around me, they agreed to let me go as long as I would let my father drop me.

"It's not safe for you to drive yet," they had all said.

I guess this was fair considering a car had taken everything away from me. I sat in the vehicle without protest as my dad drove me to my house. We both didn't have anything left to say and we sat through the journey wordlessly. Upon reaching, he quickly gave me a hug and made me promise that I would call him whenever I needed anything. I knew that I was just being given this space for a few hours and that my parents would come back to the house soon enough. I nodded in consent, knowing that I wouldn't actually be calling him.

Aryan was sitting in our bedroom with his head in his hands. I could see a half empty bottle of liquor on our bedside table. He didn't respond when I walked in and I wasn't even sure if he had noticed that I had entered. He couldn't drown his sorrows in alcohol. It only took so much time before it became a habit and we couldn't let that happen to us. I quietly went to pick up the bottle back so that I could put it back into our kitchen cabinet.

"Leave it," he replied coldly. I immediately recognised the distance in his voice.

"You're drunk, Aru. Let me keep it away, please."

"If I want to drink, I will fucking drink."

"I'm sorry this happened Aryan."

"You should be," his words took me by surprise.

"You don't mean that."

"My daughter's dead and it's all your fault."

23

July: Eleven Years after IBII

Four months had gone by since my daughter died, but things were pretty much the same. I had been eating, drinking and sleeping at regular intervals, but I performed these activities without any interest or joy. I felt like a robot being forced to maintain a routine, so that I could keep the fuel running. I was still looking for my Tahira somewhere in this big and lonely planet, knowing that she couldn't possibly be here anymore. I had seen her die in front of my eyes, but that still didn't give my broken heart enough closure. Sometimes, while I was idly sitting and thinking about her, I would wish that she was right behind my shoulder. It never came true. I liked to invent stories telling myself that my daughter wasn't really dead. She had survived miraculously and she was just sleeping upstairs in her room. She had gone off to summer camp and would be back home soon. She had joined numerous extracurricular activities and was busy learning new things. I told myself that I would see her soon, knowing that she was gone.

Taking a shower had always been the most relaxing experience for me. I think I liked them so much because I believed that they could wash off my day. They could remove the dirt and the failures and leave me clean and with hope for a better day. Immersing myself in a long and steamy shower was my way to clear my head and focus on new things. When I was in the shower, I believed that I could wash off anyone and anything. After she died, I started showering compulsively. I would go five times a day, trying to scrub off the memory of the accident. I beat my skin until it was red and aching and then I would apply body wash one more time, with the hope that it would work this time. No matter how hard I tried, I couldn't wash her away. She haunted me whether I was awake or asleep. Her voice followed me around the house and every room brought back a memory of hers. I understood why parents often moved out after their children died. It was just too painful standing in the same spot where they used to play, knowing that they would never play there again. Aryan had been of no help to me throughout my period of misery. At first, I had told myself that everyone had a different way of dealing with grief and this was just his. He needed someone to blame, and who else but his wife, who had left his daughter to die. Even though we lived under the same roof, he felt miles apart. I didn't go out of the house much, but days would go by when I wouldn't even see his face. I would stay at home and hope that his anger would ease off, and that he would be ready to confide in me. His anger was like the raging ocean, ready for a storm. It had no concern for the destruction it left behind and no remorse for what got caught in his path. It wasn't a violent anger, but a silent rage. I had glimpsed this side of him only once before, when that fool Varun had tried to kiss me at our graduation party. After having punched Varun, he hadn't said anything, but I had seen the anger brewing beneath his cool surface. That time, his anger had only lasted for an hour, but this time, I knew that it could last for months. His passion had been directed into his anger, which was directed at me. I was caught in the crossfire of him trying to deal with the loss and there was nothing I could do but wait for the anger to subside, so that the calm and sunny Aryan I knew could come back to me. I had tried to talk to him multiple times, but had always been treated as if I weren't even in the room. I was worried that he would blame me for her death for the rest of his life, and his terse words cut at me like a sharp knife.

"My daughter's dead and it's all your fault."

I had noticed the words he had used immediately. My daughter. It was almost as if he didn't even see the loss I was facing with him.

I had remained sane through the ordeal only because of one person. Radhika. She had flown back from the States as soon as she had heard about Tahira and come to our house, straight from the airport. We hadn't spoken in years, but when I opened the door to see her tear-stained face at my doorstep, suddenly everything between us had become okay. I had always taken care of her as a child. When our family toured the streets of distant lands, I kept an eye on her, making sure that she didn't stray from the path. This time around, she took care of me. The bowls of heatable food that my relatives had brought had eventually gotten spoilt and had to be thrown away. Radhika had taken up the responsibility of cleaning the house and cooking for the both of us, as well as for Aryan, whenever he was around. He had started working all days of the week and he would leave early morning and come back late, stinking of booze. Radhika claimed that she couldn't hear when he got in, but I knew that she was lying to protect my feelings. Aryan would come back at odd hours of the night and he wouldn't be quiet with his entrance. He would bang furniture and cutlery, cursing while he heated up the food Radhika had prepared. On the rare occasions that they found themselves in the same room, they were civil to one another despite knowing that neither approved of the other. Radhika couldn't stand to see the way he was handling Tahira's death and Aryan couldn't stand to be around anyone who reminded him of me. Radhika didn't care much for his animosity and had moved into the guest room without asking either of us.

"I'm going to stay here and take care of you," she had announced shifting in her luggage to the room. She came to my room to talk every night and pretended to be too tired to go back to the guest room, asking me if she could sleep with me. We both knew that Aryan would crash on the sofa and she didn't want me waking up in an empty bed.

When Savi had found out that Radhika moved in, she had heavily protested, asking me to let her stay as well. I argued that we didn't have enough room and she argued that she was willing to sleep on the floor. She had only been assuaged by Radhika's fierce commitment to protect me. Savi had then decided to spend most of her hours at my house, before and after work, only going back to her own home to sleep. I could bet that Aditya disliked me for taking her away for so long, but she refused to listen to me. I couldn't really be company to anyone and I was glad that she would spend time with Radhika and keep her entertained. My mother also tried to join us as often as she could, and the trio helped put some energy back into our lifeless house. My mother and Savi tried to help Radhika out by alternating between washing, ironing and shopping. None of them had asked what I was planning to do about Tahira's nursery yet, and I wasn't sure myself. It was the holy room of our house and nobody was allowed to enter it. Despite the absence of a lock, they knew that it was sacred. Aryan and I had an unspoken agreement that the room was ours and we would face it when the time came.

Sometimes I wondered whether Aryan got tempted to go home with another woman, while he was drinking his pain away. Although I couldn't possibly imagine him being the charming and carefree man he once was, he was still ruggedly handsome. I could almost imagine him getting swayed by some girl, but he always came back home at some time of the night and I hung onto that desperately. I knew that if I were to go to a bar now, not many men would line up. My glowing skin had become pale and tired, my lustrous hair straggly and my alluring physique frail. God knows how much weight I had lost. I would have to go out of the house soon to buy new clothes that hung on me properly, but that was a task I would take up on some other day. Tonight, I was planning on helping Radhika cook dinner. Even though she didn't mind doing the household work, she had insisted that I needed to be busier. She wanted us to cook some fancy crab dish that I didn't know how to navigate.

"Do I really have to do this?" I asked her while she boiled the crab meat.

"It's a step towards normalcy," she said handing me an onion as if it were the symbol of a revolution.

I began chopping and was interrupted almost immediately.

"Is this normal for you, Raina?"

It hadn't taken long for her to notice that I wasn't adept at the whole cooking meals thing.

"Not really. Aryan usually does the cooking," I said wistfully.

"Well, we don't know when that's going to happen again, so you might as well learn," she responded hardening her face with resolve.

I obediently followed the steps she instructed and found myself humming a tune while stuffing the crab in bread. I ate out of will and not compulsion after a long time, realising how much I had needed to keep myself busy.

"I really appreciate everything you've done for me, Radhika."

"I know I was really nasty to you. Thank you for not giving up on me."

"When you love someone, you don't give up."

24

December: Eleven Years after IBII

Happy anniversary, darling. I love you. It had been nine years since Aryan and I recited our vows to each other on the sandy beach to the calming sound of the ocean. I promise to love you till death do us part. They didn't mention whose death. I was still in love with Aryan as much as I had been that day. I doubt he felt the same about me anymore. I looked to my left and was greeted by an unoccupied pillow. Happy anniversary indeed. Once Radhika had moved out of our guest room, Aryan had taken permanent shelter there, even shifting his things from our cupboard to the room's small drawers. Work had eventually beckoned Radhika to go back. She had taken a month-long leave and she knew that she would be forced to go back to Miami once the month was over. Her boss had been sympathetic, but demanded her presence immediately. It was either that or losing her job. She had been willing to choose the latter, but I had talked her out of it. She didn't have much to do in the darkness of my home and she was wasting her potential sitting here. Her exciting job as an event manager beckoned her back. She tried to convince me to fly back to Miami with her, but I firmly refused. My life was here. Or what was left of it anyway. With Tahira gone, it felt like the energy of the house had been sucked out. It was just a semi-empty shell containing semi-empty shells of humans. People say that time heals all wounds, and I guess that is true to an extent. My daughter crossed my mind every minute of the day, but the pain had become easier to bear. I had gotten over blaming myself constantly and had accepted her death. I thanked god for the days that I got with her and chose to believe that she was only taken away from me because heaven needed more angels. As time went by, I had learnt to laugh, to dance and to sing again. I wish I could say the same for Aryan. He was as much in recluse as he had been the week of her death. I had even called his office hoping that he had found peace in his passion, but his staff had informed me that he didn't talk to any of them anymore. He was the first one to arrive and the last one to leave, but he spent all his time behind books and screens. I had also started working again. With Radhika back in the States, Savi and my mother had pleaded me to let them move in so that they could keep me occupied, but I hadn't wanted to be a burden in their lives. They both had their own houses to manage and didn't need the tension of managing me as well. They had only gotten off my back when I had promised them that I would use my time productively at office.

My first day back, I had been treated with awkward smiles and piteous eyes throughout. I couldn't take the sympathy after a while and had to leave for my house at lunch hour. Dragging myself out of home the next day, I had forced myself to go back. It had been like they were walking on eggshells around me, afraid to mention their own children or even their own happy experiences in order to not upset me. I had finally commanded them to treat me as they did before Tahira's death, informing them that I could deal with my personal issues on my own. I think they realized that their subtlety or lack thereof was making me uncomfortable and after a week, they had started talking to me normally again.

I enjoyed myself at work now, regaining my competitive spirit and necessity to do well. It was a bright environment that kept me away from the shadows of home. The thought of going back crawled in my mind at the end of every day as I took extra time finishing my last assignment. I would reach home anticipating Aryan's moods, knowing that he wouldn't come in until a few hours later. I was usually able to hear his curses from our room when he did come in. I would know the level of his alcohol intake based on the volume of his swear words. Some days, I could hear him shout 'fuck' over and over again as he stumbled across furniture. Other days, I could hear the faint sounds of him grumbling to himself as he microwaved his food. He was relatively sober those days, but the level of his alcohol intake never changed his behaviour towards me. He was always distant and cold, behaving as if I were a persistent fly that he had to swat away. It was such a shock from his usual self. He had never forgotten our anniversary and had planned flamboyant but thoughtful presents each year. I couldn't help but harbour the hope that the memory of our wedding would remind him of the love we had shared for so many years. I had bought his favourite cologne and had framed a picture of the both of us from the dinner on the night of his proposal. I rubbed my hands across the frame, sighing at our innocent smiles.

Before leaving for work I walked to the guest bedroom checking to see if he was there. He wasn't and so I dropped the gifts off on his bed sending him a text that said: *Your present waits for you on your bed.*

"Let's go out tonight! We did so much work last month, we have reason to celebrate," Shreya continued making plans even though I wasn't paying attention. She had been my assistant for two years and I had gotten especially close to her in the past year. I saw her more as my friend than the woman behind the desk outside my office. She hadn't worked with me before the accident, and didn't feel the need to mentally edit her words whilst talking about her own joyous experiences. I needed that ordinariness and I had grown to like her ambitious and funny demeanor. She was energetic and lifted the spirits of the people around her. In some ways, she even reminded me of myself before the accident.

"Rahul's event is tonight. We should go there, no? Lots of cute guys, I hear." She was also several years younger than me and enjoyed flirting and being single.

"You celebrate. I'm not in the mood."

"You're never any fun. We'll dress up and drink. It'll be good for the both of us, I promise."

"I'll see," I said half-heartedly. That was good enough for her and she went on discussing the dress she had bought recently that she wanted to flaunt.

"I wish I were as thin as you. I should really cut down on the bread," she said causing me to look down on my body self-consciously. I had lost eight kilogrammes after the accident, but had gained four back, once I had started eating routinely. Shreya was as thin as me and I rolled my eyes at her.

"You know, guys eat out of your hands. You're beautiful as you are."

"You're just being sweet so that you don't have to come for the party. How about you go back and once you realize that your night is going to be boring, you give me a call?"

"I can only go once I figure out this acquisition."

I had worked through it two times in the next hour and had no option but to go home. I tried to cheer myself up with the thought of Aryan opening my presents.

As I drove into our parking, I saw Aryan's steel grey car parked a few steps ahead of me. This meant he was at home! He barely ever got back before me and I was excited to see his reaction to the presents. The text must have made some sort of an effect on him. I walked to the guest room straight away, taking two steps at a time. It was empty and my gifts were nowhere in sight. The bedside drawers remained bare and his bathroom cabinet only contained the necessities. Where was he and what had he done with them? I closed my eyes, taking slow breaths. We were still married for a reason. He loved me and he just needed his time.

'Raina, I liked your gift.'

'Aryan?'

'Yes.'

'You liked it?'

'Yes. Happy Anniversary,' he said opening his arms. I could barely believe what I was seeing. I rushed into his arms before he had a chance to back off. I inhaled his scent, running my fingers through his hair.

'Are you surprised?'

'You haven't spoken to me in almost a year. Of course, I'm surprised,' I said with a smile that I couldn't keep off my face.

'I'm sorry baby.'

'It's fine.'

He smiled back sweetly at me and it felt like the first day when he smiled at me in the IBII canteen.

"I've missed you so much," I said out loud, wanting him to hear me even though he wasn't there.

25

I felt disgusted that I had stooped to talking to myself. Although I had imagined him finally forgiving me many times, it had never felt this real. I brushed away the tears that were about to stream across my face. Aryan had obviously come back early, seen my gifts, discarded them and left. I knew I was behaving like a crazy person, but I needed to know what he had done with them. I ran around the house, checking every room except Tahira's, but I couldn't find them. The most rational response would have been for him to simply put them back on our bed, but it lay exactly how I had left it in the morning. I went back to his room to check again. Maybe he had stuffed them in a drawer and I just hadn't noticed. I looked at his sparse drawers again, but I couldn't see the cologne or the frame. Puzzled, I walked around wondering where he could have stored them. A flash of blue caught my eye and I looked down to see the glass bottle shining from the trash can in the kitchen. He hadn't even bothered hiding them to spare my feelings. It was in plain sight, inside the garbage. I hadn't realized how much importance I had given to these gifts. I had felt that if he did keep them, it would serve as proof that he was still in this marriage with me. The fact that he had thrown them away so casually made me wonder whether he was doing the same with our marriage. Was I hanging onto a thread that was bound to break?

My phone rang and I heard Shreya's enthusiastic voice on the other end.

"Did you decide?"

"You know what? Let's do it." I found myself agreeing, even though I had picked up to inform her that I wouldn't be making it.

"I'm reaching your house in thirty."

That barely gave me any time to take a shower, choose what to wear and apply makeup. I rushed to the cubicle, going over the dresses I could wear to this formal event. As I conditioned my long hair, I realized that I was actually excited to attend the event. I used to love going out earlier and I hadn't done so in such a long time. I skimmed over all my unused gowns that had gathered dust in my wardrobe. I had an array of all colours and all types. I found a powder pink backless gown with a plunging neckline. It used to be slightly tight for me, but I had bought it as a goal dress to motivate fitness. I slipped it on and it took the shape of my body magnificently. Shreya would be here in five minutes and I still hadn't put any makeup on. I preferred an all natural look to the heavily made up models featured in magazines. I slapped some blush and lipstick on and ran to the doorway with my heels in my hands. I waited for Shreya to appear, but after fifteen minutes, I began to wonder whether she would be coming at all.

"Where are you?" I asked into my phone.

"I'm sorry, I got late choosing earrings. I'll be there in ten," she informed me. Shreya was never late to work, but that was probably because she didn't have to face the 'dilemma' of choosing earrings. I glanced at myself in a mirror and realized that my dress needed a finishing touch. Since Shreya was going to take more time, I could go upstairs and find a suitable necklace. I chose a delicate diamond pendant that complimented my dress and my daring cleavage. Deciding that I could amp up my face as well, I carefully applied mascara, making my lashes longer and darker.

"I've reached."

I walked downstairs once again, feeling nervous about the night before me. Would I fit in with the people at the event? All I knew was that Rahul was throwing the party in honour of the success of his new clothing brand. Even though I hadn't shopped there myself, I had heard my friends talk about the brand appreciatively.

As I entered the car, Shreya gaped at me awestruck.

"You. You. You have stunned me into silence."

"Look at yourself," I said, eying her beautiful black dress with cutouts at the right places.

"No, I'm serious. I haven't seen you like this. It's not only the clothes or the makeup. It's your aura. You look happier than you do on most days."

She had appeased me and I squeezed her hand gratefully.

The event was being held at the Poseidon, one of Delhi's most expensive and grand hotels. There was even a red carpet leading us to the room with all the guests. Although the lighting was dim, the gold pillars in the room stood out almost as much as the jewellery on the women. Shreya hadn't informed me exactly how rich this party was going to be and I was glad that I had chosen my gown. 'Better be overdressed than underdressed' is what my mother had told me when I was deciding what to wear for my first party and her advice had worked for me. Shreya and I fit in with the bunch of models and designers in the room. We both dropped our coats and picked up glasses of champagne as Shreya sashayed around the room greeting her friends with kisses. She was kind enough to not leave me behind as she introduced me to a whole parade of skinny and good looking girls. After half an hour of introductions, I left Shreya to order myself a drink at the bar. I finished my first gin and tonic and looked around the room to find her once again. The dim lighting wasn't working in my favour and so I resigned myself to getting another drink. After four more drinks, I felt the buzz hitting me as I swayed to the music.

"I cannot believe my eyes. It's you, Raina Kapoor."

Raina Kapoor? Nobody called me that anymore. I turned around to see a man in a neat and fitted navy blue suit. He had a light stubble with tints of grey that seemed to accentuate his brooding eyes. I had seen those eyes before.

"Armaan! Armaan Verma." I said as I stood up to hug him. At six feet tall, his figure towered over me. He clutched me in a warm embrace and I smiled at him. Armaan and I had been high school sweethearts for two years, on and off. Even though our relationship had been toxic, we were considered the couple of the batch. We were kids at the time, but the relationship had always felt intense. We were under the impression that we were in love, but we found ourselves ending it every month only to get back with teary apologies. We kept repeating the same pattern until one day we broke up, not knowing that it would be our last. Soon after, we stopped talking until we were about to part ways for college. On the last day of school, Armaan had grabbed my arm and apologised to me. This time, not to get back, but with the sole purpose of staying in touch. We had both decided that we were important parts of each other's childhoods and we couldn't let that wither away in hate and jealousy. We had promised to stay friends and had actually succeeded until well, IBII. I was seeing him after fifteen years and although he was broader and had more facial hair, he still looked like the same Armaan I had crushed on all my school life. I could see a gorgeous girl in a blue gown that was fitted till the waist and flowed waist down, looking at us. Her hair was streaked with shades of golden and brown and her makeup seemed to have been done professionally.

"Your date?" I asked nodding at her, impressed that Armaan had managed to come with someone so obviously good looking.

"Just someone I met two days back. Doesn't matter now that I've found you here. We have to catch up," he said finding a seat next to me at the bar. I had to admit, I was flattered that he was leaving a pretty young girl who seemed to be interested in him, just to talk to me.

"One Scotch for me and one vodka and Sprite for the lady," he mentioned to the bartender.

"I don't drink that anymore," I said laughing at his audacity to order a drink as if he still knew me.

"For old times' sake," he said raising his glass.

There was so much to talk about and I filled him in about my job and my marriage, forcing myself to not talk about Tahira. He told me that he had become a successful surgeon, but he still hadn't found the one yet. I told him about Shreya and how

I almost hadn't even come tonight. We covered all that we had done and all the friends that we were still in touch with over a few more drinks. I could feel myself getting light headed and I realized that mixing vodka and gin hadn't been the best idea.

"I have to say, it's been lovely talking to you tonight. I had forgotten how charming you were. You look absolutely stunning."

I giggled as blood rushed to my cheeks. Armaan knew exactly how to make women feel desirable and I'm sure he did it often.

"Do you remember, we wanted to travel to London together? Have you been there?"

"Yes, I went after high school itself. I liked the London Eye as much as I thought I would."

"You should come with me again," he said grinning mischievously.

"I'm not sure the girl in blue would like that very much."

"Those girls come and go. You and I used to be the real deal."

"Used to."

"I guess," he said, his eyes twinkling.

I looked around and realized that the party was in full swing now. People had let go of their formal and polite masks and were dancing and drinking from champagne bottles. It must be late.

"I should get going."

Armaan grabbed my hand with a certain self-assuredness.

"Your friend seems to be busy," he said glancing over at Shreya. I hadn't noticed but she was dangerously close to some man. I cheered for her mentally.

I felt Armaan pause and lean into me.

"When you talked about your husband, it sounded like things aren't going too well. What did you mean? It's been bugging me this whole time."

"I don't know if he loves me anymore," I said swallowing hard.

"Do you really think he doesn't?" he said as if he were implying that it would be impossible for someone not to. I looked into his eyes, searching as if they contained my answer.

"We haven't spoken in almost a year now."

"Did something happen?"

"Our daughter passed away and he blames me for that."

I hadn't talked about this to my closest friends and yet I found myself blurting these intimate details to Armaan.

"Fuck. That's intense, Raina. Nobody deserves that. I'm sorry."

I nodded looking down.

"What happens if things continue to be this way? Will you get a divorce?"

He had asked me the same question that had been haunting me for a while. I felt his leg press against mine as I took another sip from my drink, ignoring his question.

"Raina, I'm sure it wasn't your fault."

"He doesn't know that."

"He should give you a chance to explain," Armaan said adamantly, with heat in his eyes.

I tried to remember what he had just said, but I couldn't concentrate with him looking at me like that. I nervously looked down and fiddled with my fingers trying to think of how I could change the topic.

"He's missing out. He should be careful or someone else may just scoop you up."

He was still looking at me intently, waiting for a response.

I could feel my head spinning slightly, probably due to the excessive amounts of alcohol.

"I don't meet too many people," I said sheepishly. He took my hand in his and squeezed it gently. Good, he was just being a friend and trying to make me feel better. He slowly slid his hand on my thigh, resting it there. I could feel the coolness of his palm through the thin material of my gown. My palms started getting sweaty and my head continued to spin. He began tracing my knee with his face inches away from me. I couldn't believe that this was happening in a room in front of five hundred people. He leaned in again, brushing his lips against my cheek. I could feel what was coming next. Any second now, he would shift his mouth from my cheeks to my lips. I almost considered it for a second, but the thought of Aryan flooded my head. This wasn't the life I wanted to live.

"No." I said jerking back.

"Did I do something wrong?"

"I'm married. I need to go."

"Raina!" he protested.

"Stay away from me," I hissed at him not bothering to hear what else he had left to say.

I looked around at the crowd around us, but I couldn't spot Shreya anywhere. The dark room suddenly felt as if it could choke me and I needed to get out. I ran towards the glass doors, calling a taxi on my phone. I didn't have the patience to wait for Shreya to drop me home. I couldn't even be bothered to pick up my coat. I needed to be back where I belonged. Armaan had given me my answer, after all. I would fight for my marriage.

26

"Aryan, wake up love," I said positioning myself next to him on the guest bed. He was still sound asleep, but I needed to talk to him. I shook him gently a few more times, taking advantage of him being a light sleeper. After a few more tries, I saw his eyelids fluttering.

"Is something wrong?" he asked groggily.

Is something wrong? So much was wrong. What had happened tonight was wrong. I hadn't kissed Armaan, but I had come close to it. I needed to fess up to my mistakes. I needed to get our marriage back on the right path. I wondered if him asking me whether something was wrong was an admission of concern on his end.

"Yes. Our marriage."

"I'm not talking about this."

"We have to talk, please."

"I need time, Raina," he said turning on his side, away from me.

This was more conversation with him than what I had received in a long time and I was satisfied. I knew there was no point prodding him further, and so I walked to my room quietly and tucked myself into bed. It had been a long night and I needed the rest.

The next morning came earlier than I had wanted it to. I could still feel my head spinning as a wave of nausea swept over me. I would have to take a pill so that I could hear myself think again. I walked to the kitchen and poured myself a glass of orange juice. As expected, Aryan had left for work already. It was getting late and I knew that I would have to start getting ready for work soon. I was in no mood to hear Shreya talk about the party and my whereabouts. I had no idea how much she had seen and I didn't want to be interrogated. I decided to call in sick for work and went back to my room, eager to sleep again. The sunlight was streaming in and I groaned as I tried to shut the blinders with my useless remote. After a couple of tries, the blinders shut, successfully shielding me from the light. I set an alarm for the afternoon and shoved my head under my quilt.

"Lunch?"

"Aren't you at work?" Savi asked me suspiciously.

"I didn't go. Can I come to your office?"

"How come?"

"I was hungover."

"You went drinking without me?" Her tone went up a notch.

"I'll see you at two-thirty."

I didn't want to explain what had happened over the phone. Putting on a pair of jeans and a simple white top, I grabbed my sunglasses and car keys on my way to confide in my best friend.

Savi had picked a vintage restaurant near her office called The Italians. I hoped that the cheesy food would help soak up the alcohol in my system. To my liking, the place was decorated with couches and framed posters. The busboy guided us to a table for two next to a large window. It was a nice windy day and the street across us had come to life. Women and men scurried around rushing to go back to work or to meet their lunch dates. Some people stopped at the street shops playing with the twinkling array of earrings. There was one restaurant people seemed to be lining up for. It boasted to have the best Mexican food in the area. My stomach grumbled and I realized I was hungry after all.

"I'm going to have the vodka prawn penne. I've been thinking about it all morning, so I'm glad you asked for lunch. Do you want to have the same?"

"The word vodka is making me nauseous right now."

I looked over the large menu that seemed to have every pasta dish imaginable. The desserts page also looked tempting, but I decided to focus on that later.

"One creamy bacon carbonara and one lemon iced tea, please."

"The food here is divine. Anyway, how come you asked for lunch?"

"Something happened last night."

"Aryan forgave you?" Savi asked me enthusiastically.

My face fell at her question and she looked at me guiltily.

"I'm sorry, I shouldn't have assumed."

"It's fine," I responded absentmindedly.

"So what happened?"

I recapped the events of the night before as Savi listened patiently. We were only interrupted by our waiter when he brought over the delicious smelling dishes of pasta. I continued talking through bites of the scrumptious bacon.

"You did what?"

Savi said finally interrupting me as I reached the part of letting Armaan grab my thigh.

"It gets worse."

I finished telling her my story and she looked disappointed, not bothering to finish her dish anymore.

"I don't know what to say. Aryan isn't willing to talk to me and I've just been so lonely. I know I have you guys, but it's not the same. Being blamed for my daughter's death is a large burden and it's been so tough dealing with it. I was drunk and I felt like my marriage was going down the drain either way."

"Do you still feel that way?"

"No, I want to fight it out. I just get so unsure about his feelings at times. I get so scared that he'll blame me for the rest of his life. I should have been more careful that day Savi, what was I thinking?"

I heard Savi taking a large breath and I knew that meant that a tirade was about to come my way.

"Listen up. Firstly, what ifs aren't going to change what happened. It's horrible that it happened to you, but it could have happened to anyone. It could have very well happened on Aryan's watch. We've been over this a hundred times and I thought you had accepted that it wasn't your fault. You can do nothing to change the past, but you can change your future. You have to make sure you don't slip up again, because next time, something may actually happen. If Armaan messages or asks you to meet, ignore him. He obviously isn't a great guy since he had no qualms about hitting on a married woman. Secondly, you and Aryan are going to make it. I don't know if you know this, but I always took your relationship as an aspiration for myself. In college, I secretly hoped that I would find what you guys had. When I met Aditya, I hoped that we would last as long as you both had. When we fight, I try to imagine what the both of you would do and it usually works. When things get hard, I think of how terrible everything's been for you and your strength brings out the best in me. You cannot even think of giving up on your marriage. Think about the first time you told me that you were going to marry him. I'm not an optimist, but I believed in the both of you. I cheered for you because I knew you would make it and I still do. Think about the time you had chicken pox and he took care of you every second, even though he caught the illness himself. Think about the time Varun tried to force himself on you and he protected you. Think about all the times you picked unreasonable fights and he calmed you down patiently. I know what's happening isn't fair to you. He should have tried to talk to you instead of blaming you. I know that's true, but sometimes, when people are in pain, they need to hang onto something and he's hanging onto this. He's punishing you for what happened, but this is Aryan we're talking about and he'll get over it. He's the guy who gets you tulips now and then just to see you smile, he's the guy who plays with kids on the road, he's the guy who teaches English to the help and he's the guy who gets upset when he sees even strangers in pain. I know the wait is excruciating, but you can handle it. Give him more time to get over the pain and he will eventually come back to you. I know you guys will sort it out as long as you invest enough in the relationship for the both of you, just for a short period of time. We fall in love knowing that pain is a very real possibility. Fuck possibility, pain is inevitable. I know I sound like a quote on Instagram, but all we can do is find someone who is worth the suffering, and you goddamn know that he is. You both have to make it, because if you don't, then I don't know who else could."

27

June: Twelve Years after IBII

'I don't mind spending every day, out on your corner in the pouring rain.' The lyrics of my favourite song by Maroon 5. I had never thought that this line would be so relevant to my life, but it was. It had been six months since the Armaan incident and it was long forgotten. After the party, he had asked around and found my number.

I remember, as a college student, I would sometimes go out to clubs and talk to half decent boys. I even gave them my number if I really enjoyed their company. I never realized how superficial it all was when we were in the midst of pounding music, barely able to hear ourselves, let alone make any real conversation. Most of the boys ended up messaging with pointless one liners intended to stir conversation into meaningless directions. The conversation tended to fizzle out in a couple of weeks and it would only take me another night out to get over it. The boys that actually caught my attention were the ones that I never spoke to. I would wonder if something could have happened, had they messaged me at the end of the night. The first category was a dead end, but the second left hope for my brain to fantasise. In moments of insecurity, when I asked Charvi and Mahima why the guys hadn't reached out, they would always answer using excuses laced with optimism. He probably lost your number. Maybe he's really busy? What if he's an asshole with a girlfriend? Every excuse was essentially used, so that I wouldn't blame the rejection on myself. I knew that most guys thought that I was attractive and so it was easy for me to believe these excuses readily. Somewhere along the line, I realized that if a guy really wants to talk to a girl, he'll find a way. I had a friend that went to the same club every Saturday night until he ran into the girl whose name he did not know but had felt a real connection with. Once you had their name, it became oh so easy. You could ask around or find them on Instagram, Facebook and Snapchat in the blink of an eye. I had assumed that Armaan may use all these forms of social media to contact me and so I had blocked him in each in advance. After these apps hadn't worked for him, he had asked school friends who I had stupidly told him I was still in touch with, and stuck to iMessaging. He tried asking me to meet, so that he could apologise in person, but I had refused to reply. After two weeks of trying, he had realized that it wasn't going to happen and had given up. I had taken Savi's advice seriously and even the thought of being around him sickened me. To imagine what I had come close to doing. It would have ruined my marriage and my conscience. I despised cheaters and would continue doing so. Although Armaan wouldn't have been the cheater in that scenario, I didn't have much respect for the enabler of the cheating as well. I believed that they should have enough of an obligation to humanity to control themselves.

So here I was, humming along to 'She Will Be Loved', wondering when Aryan would love me again. I really was willing to spend every one of my days in the pouring rain if that got him to come back to me again. I had tried everything from affection to dissatisfaction to simply acting as if it didn't matter to me. Nothing had worked and I was back to affection. I just needed my husband to let go of the image he had construed in his mind and accept Tahira's death and I was willing to do all that it took. I understood where he came from. I knew that death was an inevitable part of life, but we had both assumed that we would be long gone before something happened to Tahira. The thought of death playing an active role in the life of someone our age had only struck me once when Aryan's mother had passed away during our days at IBII. Aryan had been sobbing and I had wondered how I would deal with either of my parents dying. I had known that I would need him more than anyone else. The thought of him dying had crept up in my head only for a second. I had expressed the fear to him and he had stupidly promised me that he would make sure he died after me, so that he could take care of me whenever I needed him the most, even though we both knew that it wasn't possible for anyone to live up to a promise regarding death. I wondered how I would have reacted if I were in Aryan's shoes. Would I have been able to forgive him for letting our daughter die? I know it would have taken me months to see him in the same way again. Before she died, I used to believe that Aryan would be able to protect us from any harm that came our way. But he wasn't there that day and there was nothing he could have done to take this away. I had realized that life couldn't be taken for granted and I wanted to live each day to its fullest, but I couldn't do that without my Aru by my side.

It was a rainy Sunday afternoon and I was alone at home. I usually spent my Sunday mornings volunteering at a group home that gave a second chance to girls from troubled homes. It gave the girls shelter, education, food and a support system. I loved going there every week with small presents to make their lives easier. I was currently improving their English and although it had been difficult in the beginning, they had warmed up to the idea. On my first day, they had announced that they liked nothing better than lazing around and watching television. All my attempts at teaching had been a bust with the girls who were easily distracted and eager to get back to their television set. I had then decided to start by making them watch movies that emphasised the importance of learning the language. After a couple of movies followed with heavy discussion, they had finally agreed to let me work on their grammar and writing as long as I played games with them later. The girls of different ages gave me a glimpse of what Tahira could have been like and I had grown attached to them. The NGO had organized a summer camp for them for two weeks, leaving me with an open Sunday afternoon. Knowing that nobody would be at home, I had tried making plans with all my loved ones. Aryan spending his time at his restaurant didn't come as a surprise to me, but all the others were busy too. Savi and Aditya had a family thing going on, my parents were spending their summer in Greece, Radhika was still in the States, Charvi had errands to run and Mahima was swamped at work. Apart from them, there was nobody in particular that I wanted to spend my time with. I spent the day lounging on my sofa, watching whatever semi-funny show that came on television. I definitely understood the appeal it held for the children at the home. I only took a break when I got hungry and had to prepare a meal.

Feeling too lazy to cook anything, I heated up macaroni from the night before, along with air fried chicken nuggets. For dessert, I chose to have a large serving of the chocolate cake that I had picked up on my way back home the previous week. I relished the softness of the cream combined with the crispness of the crust as I wasted another hour on the next show that aired. I was getting more comfortable in my spot and soon I found my eyes shutting despite my effort to concentrate on the scene playing out in front of me. Eventually, I crashed on the sofa with my blanket wrapped around me, while the plates holding the telltale crumbs of my unhealthy meal still lay on the table.

"Raina. Raina. Raina."

What was happening? I could hear sounds of thunder as well as Aryan's voice whispering to me. Aryan's voice? The thought jolted me awake. That couldn't be right. But there he was, kneeling in front of me.

I glanced at him, giving him a quick run over with my eyes, checking to see if he was intoxicated. Although he was wet, he seemed to be in his senses.

"Aryan?"

"Let's talk."

28

"You want to talk?" I stuttered through the question, shocked that this was happening in the middle of the night. What could have brought this on? Today wasn't a special date? It didn't hold any meaning for us. It was just one random Sunday out of so many that had gone by.

"Yes. I'm sorry."

"You're sorry?" I asked looking at him like a deer caught in headlights. I had imagined this moment a number of times, but now that it was actually happening, I didn't know how to react.

"I'm sorry I've been such an awful husband to you."

This was it. He was going to tell me he cheated on me. I could handle most things, but I refused to stay in a marriage where my husband wasn't committed to me. I braced myself for his words.

"You look scared. Oh god, are you afraid of me?"

"No, I just don't understand where this is coming from."

"I've been blaming you for something that wasn't your fault for too long."

"I should have been more careful." No! Why was I sabotaging myself?

"You couldn't have known. None of us could have. I'm sorry it took me so long to see that."

"I've been trying to reach out to you for a year-and-a-half now."

"I know," he said, his face looking ashen.

"Hira looked so much like you. Every time I looked at your face, I was reminded of hers. I was reminded of what had been taken away from me. What had been taken away from us."

"And you blamed me."

"I did. I needed someone to hold responsible. I'm sorry that it was you."

I wasn't sure whether I should embrace him as I had wanted to for so many days or address my feelings.

"I was so lonely. I had to deal with our daughter's death alone."

"I can never forgive myself for that. I promised you that I would protect you, but I couldn't even protect you from myself."

"How did you decide to forgive me all of a sudden?"

"It just struck me today. I was walking in the rain coming back home when I realized that I wasn't walking fast enough to be with my beautiful wife waiting for me. I realized that I should spend the rest of our precious time loving you and not hating you for something you couldn't control."

"You hated me?"

"I'm sorry, I hated what happened."

"How do I know you're not going to go back to that again?"

"I know you have no reason to trust me right now, but I won't. I promised you that I would stick by you through thick and thin, and I want to live up to that promise. I needed time and I thank you for giving me that. I'm here now."

I looked down not knowing what to say anymore. What if I rushed myself back into our marriage and he left me again? Would I be able to handle the disappointment and the pain? I had waited for this for so long, but now that it was happening, I was plagued with a hundred fears. Something about this didn't feel right. Was he hiding something from me?

"There's something you're not telling me," I said glancing at him to check his reaction. Now, it was his turn to look away.

"I just want to come back to you, Raina." The way he said my name… I hadn't heard him say it like that for so long.

"I'm scared."

"I know, even I am. But whatever time we do have, let's live it together without any regrets. I've already wasted too much time staying away from you."

"I missed you."

"I missed you so much, Raina. Every day I was in my room, my heart would be aching. I felt like I lost my daughter and my wife. I just couldn't face you. I know it was so unhealthy for me to bottle up all my feelings, but I couldn't talk about it. I made the same mistake when Mum passed away, except this time I felt a hundred times worse. Every time I tried, I would choke. It was easier for me to blame you than to deal with it, but every cell of my body ached with the loss. Can I hold your hand?" he asked me, his voice shaking. I could see tears welling up in the corners of his eyes. My tears had already started dripping down my face and I clumsily wiped them with one hand while thrusting my other hand in Aryan's palm.

"Let me," he said wiping my tears away with his thumb. "I should have done this for you a long time back."

A surge of feelings rushed through my body at his touch. A strange combination of love, fear, attraction, pain and longing tugged at my heart.

"Did you wait for me?" I knew he was asking whether I had been faithful.

"Yes." I would tell him the Armaan incident another day.

"I'm so happy to hear you say that."

"All those nights you came back late, I wondered whether you were with other women."

"The thought didn't even cross my mind. I was always alone, drinking in a corner. I never looked for company and it didn't come looking for me either."

"You're going to stay?"

"For as long as I can, my love," he said looking into my eyes solemnly.

"Don't hate me again," I said sobbing.

"I won't. You're my baby," he replied scooting closer to me and hugging me as I sobbed uncontrollably.

When I was finally done flooding out the tears from my system, I held his hand, leading him to our bedroom.

"Promise me that you'll sleep in this bed and not the one in the guest room."

"I promise."

"Promise me that you'll kiss me every night before you go to sleep."

A moan escaped his throat as he leant to kiss my lips.

"I promise," he whispered against my cheek. He continued to kiss my face, my shoulders and my neck repeatedly as if someone would take me away from him any second. I wrapped my body around his as I tried to stop the tears from flowing again. The fear that this moment would never happen had haunted my heart every day and it was finally happening. My imagination couldn't have compared to the feeling of actually being touched by him.

"I'm in love with you, Raina Malik."

"I'm in love with you, Aryan Malik."

29

September: Twelve Years after IBII

Having Aryan back had been the most ethereal experience after months of darkness. It was like the first glass of water after a rough drunk night. The first bite of chocolate after crash dieting for a week. The first drop of steaming hot water that drops on your back after an intense workout. The feeling of removing your bra after a long day. The feeling when you see your waiter approach your table with food. The smell of mud after rain. The one song that you and your friends sing at the top of your lungs in the car. All those feelings combined couldn't compare to having Aryan back in my life. I've seen shows where people get stuck in the middle of the ocean for days. They barely have any essentials such as food and water. They're in the middle of a storm, battling for their lives and looking for a piece of land amongst all the blue and grey. He was that piece of land for me, saving me from the horrors of the storm, and nourishing me back to life. He was my sunshine and my ray of hope. Hope for a happier life where the pain of losing Tahira didn't plague me constantly. And when I was around him, it was almost possible to forget what had happened. When we snuck in kisses at public places, ran around malls and laughed at our goofiness, it was almost like those months had never even happened. Nobody could tell that we had lost our daughter, and in that moment, we believed it too. We behaved like teenagers who had met in college and were deeply in love, looking forward to the idea of a bright future in front of us. In that moment, our daughter had never died and Aryan had had nothing to blame me for. We were just another speck in the whole wide world, ignorant towards our surroundings. Aru said he wanted to make up for all the time we had lost and so he had stopped going to work. I don't mean that he had chosen shorter hours. He had point blank stopped, assuring me that he was happier at home. Apparently, he had already appointed someone to take over the job he used to do. I thought it was a bit of a stretch, but I was ready to go along with all the decisions he made as long as I could stay in my bubble with him. Just because my husband was free, my responsibility towards office had not changed. I continued with my routine and Aryan understood, occasionally even dropping by for lunch. When I asked him what he did at home all day, he evaded the topic, saying that he had just lazed around. Aryan is an energetic person and I doubt he could stay at home all day without boring himself to death. I suspected that lazing around wasn't all he did, but I decided not to push it. He would tell me when he felt the time was right and I didn't want to say anything that would drive him away from me. The prospect still scared me, even though he promised me that it would never happen again.

The past few weeks had been amazing, but I knew that it could be taken away from me all over again. I wondered whether I should be careful and not spend all my free time with him, but when he passionately discussed the itineraries that he had made for us, it was hard to not say yes.

When I told my mother about my first boyfriend, she had said, "I know you're young right now, but don't be with someone just because you like the way they look. That's going to fade away someday, but do you know what really matters? Whether he makes you laugh. Whether he's dependable. Whether you can talk to him about your problems and whether he understands. Whether you can trust him with your words and your body. These are the things that are essential at the end of the day. His looks are going to go, but these are going to stay."

I was a teenager and I had only dated the guy because he was cute and he gave me attention. I hadn't thought of it going so far and my mother's words had taken me by surprise. That relationship ended in a month, but her words stuck with me. After that, I went over the checklist in my head every time I developed feelings for someone. Aryan was all of that and even though he had strayed from the route for a while, I trusted that he would always be those things for me.

"I have something for you," Aryan whispered in my ear, grabbing my waist.

"Show me," I said turning back to plant a kiss on his lips.

He held out a handmade book that said, 'Aryan and Raina's Day Out' with a picture of us holding hands.

"What's this?" I asked him puzzled. He wasn't too creative to begin with, but I could see the effort that had gone into the book. He had decorated the borders with ribbons and tiny gems.

"Open it!" he said eagerly.

A wide smile flew across my face as I gingerly opened it, not wanting to destroy it with my clumsy fingers.

The first page said, '12 p.m.: Breakfast in bed' with a picture of a plate full of pancakes, sausages and berries.

"This is our itinerary for the day, Raina."

"You made a scrapbook?"

"I wanted to give you something that you could keep with you physically."

"This is so sweet, Aru."

"You deserve it," he said smiling back at me.

He ran off to the kitchen to bring up my tray for breakfast. He came back in, carrying two plates and a glass of apple juice. One of the plates contained chocolate, maple syrup, pancakes and whipped cream. The other contained salami, sausages and croissants. He had heaped the food onto the plates and I knew that there was no way I could finish it alone.

"This is enough to feed a village." I laughed.

"Then it should be perfect for you. What makes you think this is only for you though? Scoot over," he said nudging me as he got under the covers.

After we were done eating, we started fooling around and I sprayed the whipped cream on his face.

"Let me make a white beard for you. Then I can decide whether I still want to be with you when we're old."

"I think I see a grey hair on your head," he teased back holding me down so that I couldn't spray him. I managed to get some on his face anyway, and he reciprocated by rubbing his face against mine. He began tickling me, which led to us kissing again. By the end of it, our faces were sticky and I had swirls of whipped cream hanging from my hair.

"This wasn't on the schedule," he wagged a finger at me, pretending to be mad and consequently reminding me of Tahira. He glanced at my expression and returned my sad smile.

"Look here, babe! Now we take a picture of ourselves and put it in the scrapbook," he said taking out a Polaroid camera.

"I've always wanted one of these!"

"I know."

I opened the second page which said, '2 p.m.: Take a shower (together)' with a picture of a bathroom selfie of us brushing our teeth in IBII.

"Subtle," I said kissing him.

I wanted to see the whole book at once, but Aryan demanded that I only open the next page once we were done with the current activity.

At four, we were done with our steamy shower and were drying each other off. I convinced him to let me open the next page so that I could dress accordingly.

'5 p.m.: Movie at Citywalk'

I was especially excited for this one. When we had just come back to Delhi, we used to go for movies to PVR every other week. We threw popcorn at the people who annoyed us and snuck in make-out sessions during love scenes. We continued going frequently, but when Tahira was born, we had to stop for a while. Raising a baby took up all our time and we only went there again to watch animated movies with Tahira. It was our family day out and we enjoyed the experience thoroughly. I hadn't gone back there since Tahira had passed away, but knowing that Aryan would be by my side made the idea a whole less intimidating.

I wore a floral bodysuit with my high waisted jeans and applied eyeliner and pink lipstick. Aryan was wearing a linen blue shirt with white pants.

"The blue flowers match your shirt."

"I guess we were meant to be," he winked at me.

We were going to watch one of those typical thriller movies where the world was going to end, but one family would be focused on to give the audience something to root for. Once we were seated with our tubs of popcorn, mine caramel and his salted, Aryan put his arm around me and I snuggled into his chest. We could see the people around us getting slightly annoyed, but that didn't stop us from whispering our versions of the plot to one another. We both made our lists of who would die and who wouldn't, competing to see who had made the highest number of correct guesses. We cheered for each of our characters and booed for the others. At the end of the movie, all of my people were alive, but two of his had died.

"I win!" I excitedly repeated myself, over and over again, as he rolled his eyes at me.

'8 p.m.: Dinner'

"Since I won, I assume I'm going to choose the place and you're going to pay?"

"Sure baby."

I guided him to a pizzeria in the mall, eager to bite into gooey and cheesy wood fired pizzas. We found an isolated booth and ordered garlic bread, pepperoni pizza and two cokes.

"Do you remember the last time we came here?"

"Of course. To watch that princess movie with Hira."

"Princess movies, my absolute favourite."

"It wasn't that bad."

"The princess couldn't compare to the two princesses I came with."

I giggled at his remark, "You're cheesier than the pizza."

"And yet you blush like this is our first date."

"You remember what she said that day?"

"Yes. We were discussing things that had to happen for us to meet. How it was almost a miracle. A miracle that we were both from Delhi, but we ended up in IBII. A miracle that you stood in front of me and a miracle that I looked into your phone. A miracle that you fell for me. All the little things that the universe ensured so that we could meet and fall in love."

"And Hira decided that that meant she was our miracle too. Because everything we did eventually led up to her existence."

"She was our miracle."

We took a picture of our pizza sticking it on the fourth page.

'10 p.m.: Ice-cream'

He had stuck an adorable picture of me licking my scoop while he sulked, because his cone had been snatched by a monkey at the zoo. I had teased him about how the monkey had recognised him as one of his own.

We drove to a gelato place on the way back home, singing all the songs out loud. Once we reached, we tried different flavours knowing that we would stick to our own either way. I chose 'Kit Kat' and he chose 'Berry Pink'. It worked for us because whenever mine got too sweet, I would steal his for the tartiness and vice versa. We asked the vendor to take a picture of the both of us holding up our cones, so that I could put it on the final page. Today had been too good to be true.

"Let's walk home?"

He parked his car in an alley near the gelato store as we walked hand in hand, licking each of our scoops.

By the time we had reached home, Aryan was panting.

"Have you not been exercising? What happened to your stamina?" I asked him slightly concerned.

I had seen Aryan climb ten flights of stairs without pausing to take a break and I was surprised that he was tired from our short walk.

"Raina, I have to tell you something," he said looking down.

It sounded serious and I could feel my heart start to beat faster.

"What is it?"

He looked straight into my eyes, holding onto both my hands.

"I'm dying."

30

I couldn't believe this was happening to me. I felt like my life had been written by Shonda Rhimes. Even Meredith Grey didn't have to go through losing both her husband and her daughter. I had spent countless hours taking in the drama of *Grey's Anatomy*. All the deaths had always seemed like a far off reality. I thought I was empathising with the characters, but I realized now, that I was only sympathising. Nobody can imagine the grief of losing their loved ones until they've been in the same situation. People can say that they understand all they want, but none of them actually do. They may think that they get it, but at the end of the day, it's not happening to them. They get to go home to their spouses and children without a care in the world. A care that actually matters in the long run, that is.

I had never seen Aryan's death coming. Maybe I should have thought about it, considering what had happened to Tahira but I had always just assumed that one great loss was enough to bear within a lifetime. If I stopped to dwell for even a fraction of a second, crocodile tears would roll out of my eyes. My wet face and salty eyes often looked up at the ceiling searching for answers as to what had I done to deserve this. Had I performed some grave sins in my past life? No sin was even comparable to this punishment.

"I noticed that something was wrong about a month-and-a half back. I had lost weight and I was feeling weaker. I decided to go for a check up, thinking it was some sort of flu. The doctor told me that I have leukaemia. It didn't sound too scary at first, but he continued to tell me that it was life threatening. He said that therapy could buy me more time, but it would have numerous unpleasant side effects. He seemed pretty firm on the dying part. I may have a few months, but I'm going to die eventually. I questioned him and accused him of giving me the wrong results. I told him that I'm only thirty-four and this couldn't possibly be happening to me. He said that he had performed the blood test three times before telling me and that there was no doubt about the matter."

"Is this why you forgave me?"

"I know I told you that I decided all of a sudden, but that wasn't the whole truth. I forgave you the Sunday I learnt about my condition. It made me realize how stupid I'd been, wasting all those months being mad, when I could spend them with you. I practically ran home so that I wouldn't spend another second being away from you," he said.

"Why didn't you tell me?"

"I didn't want the last of our time together clouded with this. You were bright and happy and this was dark and sad. I didn't want it to take over your sunshine."

"You're my sunshine, Aryan!"

"And you're my rainbow. The after effect of sunshine combined with rain. You have to be my rainbow through this. I've sold the restaurants already. There's little hope left and I start therapy tomorrow. I want you to be there with me."

"Of course. I'll leave my job today."

"Don't be silly. You have to live your life once I'm gone. Just be there whenever you can."

This wasn't a conversation thirty-four-year-olds should be having. I had to bury my daughter and I couldn't bear the thought of doing the same to my husband.

"Don't leave me again," I said weakly.

"Darling, I wish it were up to me. I was a fool to leave you the first time, but you've learnt what it is like to live without me. I need you to be happy once I'm gone. I need you to live your life for the both of us."

"I won't be happy."

"God damn it, you have to be. We're only given the lives we're strong enough to live. You're my strength and my weakness, and I know you can do this."

"Okay, I will," I said, unsure about whether I was lying or not.

31

October: Twelve Years after IBII

Therapy had started and it cost a bomb. I had told the doctors that the expenses didn't matter, but I was forced to continue working, so that I could still provide for all his treatments. I knew that if he lived for as long as I hoped, our savings would soon vanish and I would be forced to ask for loans from work and family.

The treatment was meant to slow his cell destruction, but it had terrible side effects for Aryan. His healthy blood cells were being killed in the process, harming his body's ability to fight other infections. He was always nauseous and fatigued, and the toll the disease had taken on his body was evident. The once muscular and fit human had lost ten kilos, leaving him looking lanky and weak. Even his hair had started thinning. Some days he would have swollen legs and even the smallest misdemeanours caused him high levels of bruising. Through it all, Aryan had managed to keep his spirit. His eyes still twinkled as he cracked jokes to make me laugh. And I laughed even though all I wanted to do was cry.

My boss had been sympathetic to my situation and had granted me an indefinite but paid leave until Aryan needed me. I was thankful for his loyalty and I promised to check up on the company once a week. I spent the rest of my time lying beside Aryan, or performing the activities he needed me to do. Sometimes he would just ask me to fetch popcorn so that we could watch one of the old movies coming on the hospital television. There was no recording function, but it was up to date with all the channels and we usually found something to watch.

Even though it was painful for me, Aryan insisted on talking about my future. He gave me instructions that he believed would make me happy, such as go back to work, move in with Radhika and invest in hobbies. He also insisted that I find someone else eventually and not spend the rest of my life pining over the loss.

"There's nobody else there for me, Aryan," I had whined to him, albeit his refusal to listen.

The task of telling his family had fallen to me. In all my grief, I hadn't realized that his father would be losing his child after losing his spouse as well. We were in the same boat and we often took turns to leave the room for a quick cry while the other distracted Aryan. I'm sure he knew what we were up to when we returned with red and puffy eyes, but we forced ourselves to stay strong in front of him anyway. His father had decided to move into our home and clean up while I was in the hospital. I felt guilty allowing him to do work when his son was dying, but I think the tasks helped believe that he was being helpful in his own way. I understood his helplessness because I felt the same.

All I could do was spend every waking minute with my husband and try to make him forget about the upcoming doom.

"What movie do you want to watch today, sweetheart?" I asked Aryan, climbing into his bed with snacks. He couldn't digest much and so I had stuck to simple strawberry jelly.

"No movie today. I just want to hold you."

I lay my head on his chest and listened to the beat of his heart. I prayed that his heart would beat for a long time.

"Thank you, Raina."

"For what?"

"For giving me the best life I could have possibly asked for."

"My world revolves around you, Aryan. It's my job to make you as happy as I possibly can."

"And you have. You've made me the happiest man on earth," he gently kissed my forehead, closing his eyes.

"Why are you acting as if this is it?" I said scrunching up my face, so that I wouldn't start crying.

"I want you to smile," he urged me and I painted a fake smile on my face.

He grabbed my waist, leaning in to tickle me and I couldn't help but flash him a real smile.

"That's my girl."

I kissed him on his lips and he sighed, breathing in my hair.

"I love you," he whispered his last words in my ear.

Epilogue

November: Twelve Years after IBII

I had immersed myself into staying busy at all times. You have to do what Aryan wanted you to do. He wanted you to be happy. I told myself this every minute of the day as I forced myself into yet another task that I really wasn't in the mood for.

"Eat your meals regularly," his voice rang in my head as I heated up the waffle my mother had made for me.

I had just taken a bite when bile rushed up my throat, causing me to run to the bathroom. Nausea and headaches had become parts of my daily routine, accompanying me when I woke up and when I went to bed. I scrounged through the drawers, looking for tissues, when my eyes fell on an unopened packet of sanitary napkins. I began to calculate how long it had been since my last period. Aryan had passed away a month ago and I couldn't remember the last time I had had my period when

I was with him. I opened the notes application on my phone where I carefully recorded my cycle. My last period had been in September. It had been two months already. This couldn't be possible. I knew I had a pregnancy test lying around from the time Savi had wanted to check. I peed on the stick, too impatient to sit and wait for the results. Checking my watch continuously, I forced myself to push away all the hopes I had already started to harbour of a second child. Aryan's child. The perfect symbol of all that he had given me.

I finally allowed myself to glance at the test result and a plus sign stared back at me.

I was pregnant.

Recommended Reading

LOVE A LITTLE STRONGER

This book is a collection of moments and memories, which make up the rich fabric called *LIFE* – the tiniest of things that brought us joy, the small moments that made us feel loved, and those that left us worried.

Bursting with her hilarious narratives, poignant observations and a writing style loved by millions, this book is certain to strike a chord with anybody who has children or who has been a child! Based on the author's life experiences, it teaches us to never give up on our families or life and to *Love A Little Stronger*, no matter what happens.

ISBN: 9789387022133; Pages: 176; MRP: INR 175/-; Binding: Paperback

LIFE IS WHAT YOU MAKE IT

Ankita Sharma is young, good-looking, smart, with tons of friends and boys swooning over her. Six months later, she is a patient in a mental health hospital.

It's a story that makes us question our beliefs about ourselves and our concept of sanity, and forces us to believe that life is truly what one makes it.

ISBN: 978-9380349305; Pages: 224; MRP: INR 150/-; Binding: Paperback

PREETI SHENOY *is the bestselling author of* Life is What You Make It *and seven other titles. Her books have been translated into several languages. She is amongst the highest selling authors in India. She is also a speaker, columnist and artist.*

ALL YOU NEED IS LOVE

Neil and Gauri have made it big and are living a happy life with their daughter Neilakshi. It is when they go missing in Cuba on a business trip that we begin to wonder who would want to pull them apart. Or murder them?! The hostile lover, a long lost obsessive girlfriend, or something much bigger? The mystery deepens in this final part of the 'Messed Up!' trilogy.

ISBN: 9789387022423; Pages: 176; MRP: INR 175/-; Binding: Paperback

LOST IN LOVE

Neil has been dumped by Arya and he is shattered. Gauri, who has had a crush on him forever, walks in and makes things turn around. This is a heart-wrenching romance thriller is bound to move you and hit your soul as you take a plunge and get *Lost in Love*.

ISBN: 9789387022119; Pages: 176; MRP: INR 175/-; Binding: Paperback

MESSED UP! BUT ALL FOR LOVE

Neil and Gauri are married and well settled in Gurgaon. Drishti is a journalist who gets abducted and Neil is framed for it. Her husband is a top cop who wants to dig deeper, and Gauri leaves Neil. In their messed up lives, will love make a difference?

ISBN: 9789382665946; Pages: 176; MRP: INR 175/-; Binding: Paperback

ARVIND PARASHAR *is an author and painter hailing from Dehradun. He has been a corporate leader in various firms like GE, Dell and Genpact. He enjoys road trips and gives motivational lectures at various educational institutes.*

A GIRL TO REMEMBER

Neil is a self-proclaimed demon, who has the charm to win hearts and the plan to steal them too. Annu is a stunning independent woman, who is wise and craves some love. It is with Neil that things start looking brighter, but then there's Pihu too, a confused and over-emotional teenager.

Within the entanglements of this triangle of desire, need and obsession, will love find a way?

ISBN: 9789387022393; Pages: 224; MRP: INR 195/-; Binding: Paperback

HER LAST WISH

He sees himself as a failure in life till he marries a charismatic girl. Everything is going per plan, till he finds out that she does not have much time to live. *Her Last Wish* is an inspiring story of love, relationships and sacrifice, which proves once again how a good wife makes the best husband.

ISBN: 9789382665878; Pages: 208; MRP: INR 175/-; Binding: Paperback

YOU ARE THE BEST WIFE

This is a story about how Ajay and Bhavna meet and fall in love, while destiny had some other plans. Would Bhavna's leaving him forever mean the end of love?

ISBN: 9789382665540; Pages: 248; MRP: INR 175/-; Binding: Paperback

An IT engineer who writes stories of love as his passion, **AJAY K PANDEY** *has touched the lives of many with his writing. His bestselling books* You Are the Best Wife *and* Her Last Wish *have been on top of various bestseller charts, while* A Girl to Remember *opened at #1 bestseller in pre-orders itself.*